LAST MAN STANDING

(Matt Drake #8)

by

David Leadbeater

Copyright 2014 by David Leadbeater

ISBN:9781500789127

All rights reserved. No part of this publication may be reproduced, distributed, or transmitted in any form or by any means, including photocopying, recording, or other electronic or mechanical methods, without the prior written permission of the publisher/author except in the case of brief quotations embodied in critical reviews and certain other non-commercial uses permitted by copyright law. All characters in this book are fictitious, and any resemblance to actual persons living or dead is purely coincidental.

Other Books by David Leadbeater:

The Matt Drake Series

The Bones of Odin (Matt Drake #1)
The Blood King Conspiracy (Matt Drake #2)
The Gates of Hell (Matt Drake 3)
The Tomb of the Gods (Matt Drake #4)
Brothers in Arms (Matt Drake #5)
The Swords of Babylon (Matt Drake #6)
Blood Vengeance (Matt Drake #7)

The Disavowed Series:

The Razor's Edge (Disavowed #1)
In Harm's Way (Disavowed #2)
Threat Level: Red (Disavowed #3)

The Chosen Few Series

Chosen (The Chosen Few trilogy #1)
Chosen 2 Coming September 2014

Short Stories

Walking with Ghosts (A short story)
A Whispering of Ghosts (A short story)

Connect with the author on Twitter: @dleadbeater2011

Visit the author's website: www.davidleadbeaternovels.com

Follow the author's Blog
http://davidleadbeaternovels.blogspot.co.uk/

All helpful, genuine comments are welcome. I would love to hear from you.
davidleadbeater2011@hotmail.co.uk

DEDICATION

For all the writers who weaved their words and captured me, from an early age, within their wonderful webs:

Enid Blyton, Franklin W. Dixon, Graham Masterton, Stephen King, Peter Straub, Stephen Donaldson, JRR Tolkien, David Eddings, Terry Brooks, HP Lovecraft, Robert E. Howard, Robert Crais, Andy McDermott, Douglas Preston & Lincoln Child, James Rollins . . .

LAST MAN STANDING
(Matt Drake #8)

by

David Leadbeater

CHAPTER ONE

If the last year or so had taught him anything, it had taught Matt Drake that to stay on top of things he had to act quickly, and that despite the fact that some people were beginning to think he might indeed be a one-man disaster area, to dwell and tarry and hope for the best could end up costing his friends, and occasionally the rest of the planet, everything they held dear. If fate had chosen him to be the world's soldier of fortune, its ready champion, then so be it.

With these thoughts still half-formed in his mind he dropped everything the moment he walked out of Hayden's hospital room and turned to Mai.

"Ben's funeral is in four days," he said. "In Leeds, Yorkshire. That gives us time to fly to Russia, search Zoya's place, and then attend."

Mai only shrugged. "After all the talk of this supposed tournament invite, I thought you may want to remain here and see if Coyote contacts you too."

"Let's take the bitch by the horns," Drake said. "This tournament could all be a load of bollocks, but know for a fact that Zoya was in contact with Coyote on behalf of the Blood King. We'll worry about this supposed tourney and our bloody non-existent invitations another time."

Mai sighed. "If that's what I have to do to get some alone time with the man of my dreams then let's go. Now."

"My thoughts exactly. Almost."

"But what about me?"

Drake turned to see the eighteen-year-old Grace standing behind Mai. "Hey, I can think of a million reasons why you should stay put. The Japanese are trying to find your parents. They're trying to find *you*—who you are. Your memory loss is being addressed. You're safer here. We don't know who might be looking for you."

Grace pouted. "That's five at best. Not a million."

Mai crouched down and laid a hand on the young girl's shoulders. "It is best you stay, *koibito*. The authorities may need your help too. We won't be gone for long."

"All right." Grace's face showed that she already understood the reality of the situation and had been playing Drake. Wiser than her years, this girl had potential. Drake berated himself for thinking of her as a possible asset, rather than a victim that should be reunited with her parents.

"So who's best to hang with around here?" Grace wondered. "The soldier Smyth likes Mai but tries not to show it. He likes Lauren too, but in a different way." The young girl almost blushed. "He's cool though. Kinimaka and Hayden are into each other, and always seem lost in each other. What of Yorgi? He seems okay, too."

Drake made a face at Mai. "Not sure I'd recommend any of 'em for looking after an eighteen-year-old, love. Probably best on your own."

Mai narrowed her eyes at him. "They're *all* responsible," she said. "You may depend on everyone and learn from what they share. Except Smyth," she added. "Ignore him."

"And what will your colleagues think when they find that you have left them?"

"Our colleagues . . ." Drake nodded at the closed hospital room door. "Will understand."

Entry into Russia was a tad easier of late, what with Putin sticking the majority of his nose into the Ukraine and the rest of the country becoming distracted. A White House call to a friendly Russian controller ensured a flight got the green light without delay. Funds may have been exchanged, possibly even a vehicle, but none of that troubled Drake and Mai. Their mission was clear and precise, and had to be carried out speedily. By the time the wheels squealed their greeting to Russian tarmac, the pair were donning equipment; and even before the doors were opened Drake was cajoling the pretty stewardess to just let him do a 'jump-and-roll'.

Mai managed a lot of eye-rolling at his back.

The stewardess kept it together admirably, remembering her health and safety training, and finally allowed them to disembark with a happy smile. A priority customs check and a fast car had them close to Zoya's place in good time, and Drake found that he could finally relax.

"So," he leaned back in his seat and spread his knees, "wanna hop aboard?"

Mai raised her brows. "I don't believe our driver would approve, do you?"

"No worries. I don't think he speaks English. Or Japanese. Besides, we'll make it quick."

"Don't be a goof. You know what I mean."

Drake sighed. "I guess. But, you know, since we got back together." He spread both hands. "Hasn't been a whole lot of *us* time available. Too busy saving the world."

"You don't remember that waterfall on the island near Korea?"

"Sounds more romantic than it actually was. But yeah, there are certain parts that stick in my mind."

"Then what? You getting soft on me, Drake? Don't tell me you want to start doing it in an actual bed?"

"I'd never go soft on you, Mai," Drake said with a straight face. "And didn't I just offer to do it right here?"

"Perv."

"I should know by now that I'll never win."

Mai smiled. "There you go. You have discovered the first step to a healthy relationship."

"Japanese proverb?"

"Female proverb."

"But seriously." Drake placed a hand over hers. "Maybe we should take some time. Soon. Since we're based in the US we'll call it a vacation. A road trip. Whatever."

Mai stared into the middle-distance, her expression suddenly hard. "You're right about one thing. We should talk. I did something in Tokyo to a largely innocent man, something I now regret. It haunts me."

"So let's talk it through."

"'Talk it through'," Mai echoed. "I murdered a man, Matt. To help find my parents. Gyuki made me murder a money launderer."

Drake knew enough to say nothing at first, but then he said, "Triad?"

"No. Not Triad. Not exactly. Look, we're here. Let's do this another time."

"Sure."

Their Russian driver threaded the vehicle carefully through the bulk of Zoya's property. Drake stared out the window and took in the sights, recalling the crazy assault, the fences and shattered guard towers, the trees that had secreted booby-traps, and the front porch where the crazed behemoth had spectacularly missed the most important kick of her life.

The silence between the couple stretched until their driver pulled up outside. Mai exited quickly, making Drake scramble to follow her. The Russians had said they'd already cleared Zoya's place, sure, but both Drake and Mai knew from experience that Russian-built products and promises weren't perfectly reliable.

Drake drew a handgun, an FBI issue Glock that rather surprisingly didn't employ a contemporary safety, and hissed at Mai to tread carefully. The Japanese woman ignored him, crossing the threshold into Zoya's house with only a cursory check. After that, however, she slowed down. Drake motioned to the right.

"Wonder if those cookies are still in the oven?"

Mai used her senses to test the new environment. "We're alone," she said. "Let's get busy."

Drake pocketed the Glock, having complete faith in her. "All right. Should we start with the treasure mountain?"

"Where else?"

Through another door, the great improbable pile of loot sat largely undisturbed. The Russian machine still moved slowly it seemed, thank God. Drake blessed Moscow's snail-pace bureaucracy, not for the first time in his career.

"You know," he said, "the US should inventory this entire house whilst the Russkies are still flogging king of the hill with people's lives over in the Ukraine. Who knows what treasures, what secrets, are buried in here?"

Mai nodded. "No argument there."

With time ticking away they got down to do what they came for. Carefully, gingerly, they picked at the pile, discarding swords, Uzis, a whole chest full of mixed-up bullets, mortar shells, anti-tank guns, grenades in bunches like deadly pineapples, and more guns than even Drake could keep track of.

Several of which looked futuristic.

"I'll give this to Zoya," he said. "Girl sure knew how to party."

"Not sure what you mean by that," Mai said distractedly. "All I see around me is death and madness."

Drake frowned. Something had certainly changed within Mai, and it had a lot to do with Tokyo. He saw her reading a leather-bound book. "What you got?"

"I'm not sure. Something about a *Lionheart Treasure*. Maybe for the future."

Drake agreed. "Yeah. I keep seeing tomes relating to Pandora, plagues and there's a newish pad here about something called the Pythians. And the Devil's Pyramid. What the hell is that? I think if we don't stay on topic we could be here for days."

"Weeks," Mai said. "So look out for Coyote, Kovalenko, Blood Vendetta. Stuff like that."

"Last Man Standing," Drake said, putting the pad aside. "That's the name of the supposed tourney."

Mai was plucking more distracting volumes out faster now, revealing even more treasures at the heart of Zoya's pile. A bulky black chest, strapped down with leather fastenings and three enormous padlocks. A brass plate screwed to the top read: *Le Comte De Saint Germain.* Mai's eyes widened to saucers, but she made herself ignore the huge chest, flicking through a sheaf of papers piled to its side.

"Nothing," she said. "Nothing and nothing."

"Bollocks," Drake agreed with Yorkshire aplomb. "Bollocks and more bollocks. Look, Grannyzilla must have had a laptop or something. How else could she have communicated with Kovalenko's lieutenants?"

Mai pursed her lips. "Could be. You go look for that. I'll continue here."

Drake rose, trying not to groan as the toll of the past year manifested itself in the deep aching of his joints and muscles. The sudden thought of pain brought forth an onset of guilt—at least he was still alive to feel this variety of emotions, unlike some of the heroes that had fallen along the way.

Take a moment.

After a while he moved out of the room, casting a searching eye around the kitchen. Zoya's idiosyncrasies meant that a laptop could be hidden literally anywhere. Hang the rule book, the Russian monster had been an utter loon. The oven was the first place he looked, perhaps with more curiosity than expectation. Burned cookies stared back at him, their little charred faces drooping; a sight that filled him with a sudden unaccountable sadness.

It made him think of children, and all that he had lost in his life.

The tray had warped a little. Drake pulled the cookies out and placed them on top of the stove. The Russian driver, smoking a cigarette in the doorway, stared at him strangely.

Drake shrugged and turned away, quickly opening cupboards and checking shelves, then standing on top of chairs to inspect the harder to reach alcoves and hideaways. Dust dens and spiderwebs greeted him. Pretty soon, he crossed into the front room and began an inspection there. When the hunt still revealed nothing he gave an audible groan and went to find Mai.

"Damn. I got nothing. There's only one place left to search. Do you fancy . . ."

Mai smiled sweetly. "Not a chance. Have fun. Oh, and be careful. Zoya was probably sexually active."

Drake closed his eyes. "Thanks for that."

He made his way warily to the woman's bedroom. The big double bed was unmade, the dirty sheets rumpled. He tried to dismiss the sight of rubber-boot prints on the duvet at the foot of the bed. Such visualizations could lead to debase imaginings. The drawers were full of clothes, but at the bottom of the wardrobe, hidden by hanging coats and trousers, he found a sparkly new Lenovo.

Within a minute he had it laid out on a table and was calling Mai. The Japanese woman came through to see the welcome screen flashing up.

"Good luck with the password."

"These days," Drake said. "With Windows 8, most people leave their accounts logged in just as they do on their mobile phones. It's quicker. I'm hoping . . ."

The front-page apps showed which e-mail account Zoya used most and flipped nicely open when Drake clicked on it. "Thank you, app developers," he said. "For making all our accounts so much easier to access."

Mai jabbed at the screen. "That folder there. DK. Dmitry Kovalenko. You know, until now, I actually thought this might be a huge waste of time."

Drake opened the folder. Immediately half a dozen e-mails flashed up, all entitled *Blood Vendetta*. Drake quickly checked the 'sent' folder and noted that every single one had been forwarded. Zoya then was indeed the go-between, acting as a middle-monster between Kovalenko and Coyote.

He clicked on the last e-mail, scrolled to the bottom and started to read the exchanges. The contents were stark and grueling, sent at the Blood King's behest for the attention of the world's greatest assassin. Drake expected ghastliness and was not disappointed.

Mai read it without emotion. "It changes quickly from an exploratory message sent to Zoya that appears to contain several . . . code words?"

Drake nodded. "Yes. Some kind of security protocol that even then is vetted by the Russian before being forwarded to Coyote. But once established—" he didn't need to continue.

"Yes, it's pretty graphic. There's a request from Kovalenko's men to bring Coyote in, in the event of his death. It actually says 'finish the job', and 'activate in the events of Dmitry's death'. It's real." Mai hung her head. "Damn. I can't believe that after all this, and with the bastard dead, this is all real."

Drake linked her fingers. "Coyote was always going to be an obstacle that at some point would need addressing," he said. "This way, we don't get to put it off. We take her on directly."

"So the big question, the one everyone's been asking since Odin . . ." Mai left it hanging.

"Who is Coyote?"

"Yeah. I'm betting it's Alicia."

Drake didn't smile. "Don't forget what Coyote has done."

Mai bowed almost imperceptibly. "Sorry."

"It's fine. But what we have here, what we really have in a crazy way—is the first real proof that Coyote exists. And a way to backtrack. All we have to do is find out where Coyote's e-mails originated from."

Mai could have doused his sudden fire with a flood of pessimism, but chose not to. Drake silently thanked her. He knew the chances of her using her own personal channels were practically zero at the moment. But there was another problem.

"Damn. We can't ask Karin, can we? Bollocks. She'd have this cracked in about ten minutes."

"Is there anyone else?"

Drake let out a breath. "Yeah. Of course. Dozens of people. Hundreds, probably. We do have the resources of the US government. But—" he shook his head. "Someone I would trust with information like this?"

He fell silent. Mai watched his face. Something this important, this sensitive, required a Karin or a Ben. Or even a Jonathan Gates. A proven trustworthy warrior that could be relied upon to do it right. Truth be told, Mai couldn't think of a single person.

Then Drake looked up. "There is one person. Just one man I would trust with this."

Mai frowned. "Who?"

"Michael Crouch."

Drake walked out into the sunshine, leaving the sense of cloying madness behind, and thought about what he would say. Crouch had contacted him recently, probing for information, and Drake hadn't exactly come through. But the Yorkshireman knew that the boss of his former boss was not one to hold a grudge, but one highly principled and disciplined straight arrow.

He made the call and waited for Crouch to become available.

Eventually the clipped tones leapt across the airwaves. "Drake? How the devil are ya?"

"Not bad, sir. And how's the Ninth?"

The Ninth Division was the covert British agency with blanket authority to protect England's assets anywhere, at any cost.

"Still here. And kicking arse like the Good Samaritan's hysterical donkey."

Drake remembered now that Crouch was prone to adding the occasional over-embellishment in his descriptions. Doing so now meant the boss of the Ninth Division was enjoying a slow day.

"We need your help."

"What can I do?"

Quickly, Drake outlined the situation, not surprised when he heard Crouch's sharp intake of breath on hearing the name of Coyote.

"So we have a chance to nail this Jackal." Crouch rarely made accidental references. To call Coyote by that name showed both the hate and regard in which he held her. "Just give me a minute."

Drake felt Mai come up beside him and knew, even as she laid her head on his shoulder, that she was scanning the area for adversaries. The bane of their brilliance was that they could never switch off.

"Drake? You there?"

"Yes, sir."

"Send the files over. Send them here. I have someone that can do all kinds of shenanigans, an outsider actually. And Caitlyn – that's her name – could never be back-traced. She sure speaks the lingo. Remote capture of your laptop. Piggybacking. Backtracking through digital trails. I won't pretend to understand it all, but she'll get the job done."

"Excellent. I'll send the file and leave the laptop turned on then. Will that do?"

"Probably." Crouch laughed. "Give us an hour then call back."

Drake ended the call. "Now, we wait."

"It will give us chance to talk."

"About what?"

"Oh, so much. How Dai Hibiki is looking into Grace's past and trying to track her parents. How the DC doctors are trying to jog her memory using a kind of hypnosis. How I murdered a man, a father of two, in cold blood and, one day, expect to pay for it. How even changing my phone number doesn't stop Smyth from texting me. How Alicia will cope now, and what she'll do. This is the aftermath, Drake. Everything changed when Kovalenko hit DC. What do we do next?"

"Next? I have no idea. I'm living day to day. Aren't you?"

"We all are. But that can only last so long."

Drake took a while to think it through. "You know what I think? The catalyst is Hayden. Always was. When she gets better, we'll have somebody we all respect to lead the way."

Mai thought about that. "It makes sense. But Drake, it's going to take something big to stop this team from breaking up. Something bigger than anything we've encountered so far."

"Is that even possible?"

Mai shrugged. "I don't know."

They talked some more, carefully avoiding Mai's most dangerous problem, as if knowing that an hour was just nowhere near enough time in which to tackle it. The time ticked by and the Russian driver smoked until Mai worried he might very well expire on the spot.

As the late afternoon sun began to fall from the skies, Drake's phone rang. "I'm here."

The line was silent, uncharacteristically so. Drake checked to see if the line had gone down. "Are you there, sir?"

"Yes." Crouch's voice was low, devoid of fire, of confidence. The man sounded as if the whole world had just come crashing down around him.

"Did you manage to discover the origin of those e-mails?"

"Yes. Yes we did."

Drake felt a little like a man trying to kick-start a dead horse. "Where do they originate from?"

Crouch's voice dropped yet another octave. "God help us, Drake. They were sent from here. From the Ninth Division."

A 747 landing on his shoulders couldn't have surprised Drake more. His mouth fell open and he adopted similar mannerisms to what he imagined Crouch must be displaying thousands of miles away.

"It can't be. No way. From *the Ninth*?"

Drake stared at Mai, utter incredulity shining from his eyes. But he knew better than to question Crouch any more. The man made little or no statement that hadn't been properly verified.

"It gets worse." Crouch groaned, his words forced from his throat like daggers. "The e-mails were sent . . . from Shelly's computer."

Drake stiffened again. Shelly Cohen was and always had been one of the mainstays of the Ninth Division, ever since its long-ago inception. Known affectionately as Crouch's vice chairman, she regularly stood in for the boss and undertook missions of her own.

"Someone set Shelly up?" he said immediately. "Why would they do that?"

"I don't know," Crouch said. "The protocols are pretty strict, but I guess it could be done. Either way, Drake, it's an inside job. Has to be. The e-mails originated from our intranet."

"Gotcha. So what does Shelly say?"

"Don't know. She took a week's holiday two days ago."

An inexplicable shiver ran down Drake's spine. "She did? Christ, that's unfortunate."

Crouch didn't answer. Drake knew what he was thinking. "But *Shelly*?" he said. "She's always been part of the backbone. The lifeblood. Shelly is . . . well she's at least four parts of the Ninth Division."

"And has always had access to every piece of Intel the British government ever acquired."

Drake shook his head. "All right then. Why now? Why does this operative, so good she's worked under the radar for twenty years, suddenly make a rookie mistake?"

Crouch remained silent, waiting.

Mai fixed him with a challenging stare.

And then Drake got it. "That's the whole point isn't it? Coyote *is* too good to ever get caught. This was a deliberate act."

"I believe so."

"Kovalenko must have paid her a fortune. Jesus, sir, we have to be sure. Have you tried raising Shelly?"

Crouch exhaled. "Of course I have. Every channel. No answer so far. We won't give up on her, Drake, until the proof is absolute. And at that time . . . I'll be happy to slit her throat."

Drake still couldn't reconcile the facts. Coyote had killed Alyson. Coyote was the world's greatest and worst contract killer. Assassin. Cold blooded murderer.

Shelly?

"I . . . I need time with this, sir. Let me know what you find."

"Of course," Crouch said and signed off. As he did so Drake thought he heard a gunshot.

CHAPTER TWO

As Michael Crouch ended the call to Drake a shot rang out behind him. Shocked, he turned, already reaching for the handgun kept in the drawer by his side. The Ninth Division offices near London were kept intentionally sparse. The various chiefs, cyber experts and field-soldiers were in a constant state of flux, always shipping in and then out to the next crisis. Just this month Crouch himself had overseen jobs in Vienna, Zurich and Milan. The world was always warding off a catastrophe of some sort. The room was rectangular, a low-roofed shed with multi-colored exposed cables, thickened walls, expensive computers balanced on the edges of cluttered desks, operatives rolling along at hyper-speed on their castor-fitted chairs, locked and barred weapons cupboards, and privacy corners set apart only by curtains. The Ninth Division had always been rough and ready, poised to act in an instant and used to the constant comradeship and tramp of soldier's boots; the knife-edge of Britain's response, the rugged home and op-center of military men.

It was, however, set in the middle of a small regimental compound, surrounded by electric fences and surveillance systems and guards with guns. For someone to breach the security this far it had to be an . . .

. . . insider job.

Crouch saw a cyber-information analyst go down, a man he'd trained for eight years. He flinched as blood splashed across a screen. The person shooting was definitely not Shelly Cohen. It was a hired merc, ex-Army, clad in body armor and full-face helmet, but easily recognizable to seasoned men like Crouch because of the way he fired his weapon and conducted himself. Within seconds more men had appeared behind the first, squeezing off careful shots.

Warning shouts came through the comms. *Yeah, thanks,* Crouch thought. *About as much fucking use as a four-cylinder Ferrari.* Calmly, he took in his immediate surroundings, logging the young, capable and extremely loyal soldier, Zack Healey, ducking across from the left, and the heavy-boned, craggy-faced Rob Russo rumbling over from the right.

A good, hard line.

Crouch raised and sighted his gun. "Did you call it in?"

Healey replied, "I was already consulting with Armand Argento from Interpol, sir. He's taken the reins."

"Good man." Crouch knew Argento was one of the best. "Now let's thin the herd a bit."

The three men opened fire, bullets striking true about the chests and heads of their attackers. Grunts and howls announced their agonies, but the ones with chest-shots only staggered and looked meaner.

"Bloody body armor," Crouch declared.

"We have armor-piercing bullets behind the bars, sir," Healey said, looking eager.

Crouch weighed up the options. He counted at least a dozen adversaries inside, and God only knew how many more waited outside. But up against that was the sanctity, the eminence and reputation of the Ninth Division. Crouch would not let it slip away so easily.

"Go. They hit us in our house, we'll slice their goddamn heads off with paper cuts if we have to."

Healey scrambled away on all fours. Bullets laced the air in his wake. Unfazed, the young soldier reached the far gun cabinets and punched in a quick four-digit code. Crouch watched anxiously, still tracking his enemies and staying low. Shots flew all around them. A mug full of coffee was shot to bits, sending its hot contents all over him. Great, now to add insult to injury he smelled of cheap, instant brown sludge.

The mercs advanced as a practiced unit. Healey slid a full box of ammo clear across the smooth wooden floor, passing through chair legs and under desks, right to Crouch's feet.

Russo dived right in with him. "Kid's got Olympic champion potential for box sliding at least."

Crouch exchanged the standard rounds for the more powerful ones in seconds. Then he rose and fired a salvo. The mercs, arrogant behind their armor, were advancing hard, firing consistently. Crouch saw techs struggling for cover and professional British soldiers pinned down. Then his bullets made their mark, sending the oncoming team to their knees with shouts of fury. Blood leaked and pumped through their vests. Other men stood over them, shotguns now raised, but Russo took them out in the next few seconds and soon Healey was joining in from the far left. A stray shot passed by Russo's face, making the man flinch, but Crouch figured his fellow soldier was so heavily boned up top that the slug would either bounce off or simply disintegrate into metal dust. His eyes flicked toward the yard monitors just above his head and locked onto the single one that hadn't been shot to bits.

"Shag it off," he said.

Russo looked at him. He'd heard the boss utter that phrase enough times to know what it meant: *Get the hell out.*

"Dozens of them," Crouch said. "This crew is only the advance team."

Rather than a daring raid Crouch now knew that this was an extermination. No warning bells had sounded. No alarms. Not even a shout. Somebody knew the position of every guard, every camera. Every computerized failsafe.

Somebody . . .

Crouch backed away. As much as he felt a chest-full of anger and determination, he still struggled with the absolute shock of betrayal. And not from just anyone—from the one person he had considered his best. Even worse was her status as a master assassin and her ability to operate right under his nose.

Maybe it was time to hang up the guns and don the slippers; time to concentrate on that other endearing love of his life— archaeological mystery.

But now he grabbed the box of ammo and rushed over to the far wall. Healey grinned at him, all boyish excitement. Damn, he needed a hard man or woman to curb that boy's fire. It was either that or the daft kid would get himself killed.

Daft kid? Crouch thought. *More like one of the youngest proven soldiers in my regiment.* Was he really getting too old for this shit?

Russo dashed up behind. Crouch turned to gauge the positions of his other men and women. All were ready, prepared to fight. As he lifted his arm, preparing to move, there came an almighty crash as if the whole shed was falling in, collapsing on top of them. Crouch saw two grappling hook arms break through the shorter wall, then burst open as they sensed space or air, each one deploying four grappler arms and digging back into the wall of the shed.

"What in the name of astounding warfare is that?" Crouch whistled.

"Nothing good," Russo said. "Not for us."

A sudden jolt rocked them all off balance. The entire prefabricated shed shuddered, and Healey pointed out a fact that Crouch really didn't like.

"You realize the floor is a part of this structure, don't you? It's bolted and welded to the base of the walls."

"They just plonk these things down wherever we go," Crouch said, "if they can." Then he looked around. "Brace yourselves."

Another stomach-churning lurch and one of the grapplers looked as if it was about to tear its way back through the wall, then the whole shed shifted. Desks grated and displaced their burdens. Computers, phones, files and drawers crashed to the floor. The shed stirred one more time, throwing Healey to the ground amidst the clutter. Then, suddenly, as Crouch reached down to help Healey up, the shed heaved and pitched, then faltered forward as if being dragged.

It picked up speed.

Crouch stumbled. The shed yawed. A grating noise like the slow opening of the world's most rusted gates made him want to cover his ears. The entire structure was moving and there was nothing they could do about it.

At least, that was Crouch's first fleeting impression. Once that ridiculous moment of weakness passed, he applied himself to the actual problem.

How to get out of the moving office.

He pictured the geography of the area around them. The shed had been put down on the outskirts of an industrial park, alongside electrical-goods outlets, builder's merchants, conservatory retailers and blocks of brass-name-plate offices. Directly in front of them was a barely used airfield. Beyond that a steep grassy bank and the Thames.

Crouch reeled back as the shed shook again, threatening to come apart. In his heart of hearts he actually doubted that would be a good thing. Their enemies probably had many weapons readied for just that scenario. He flinched as a lampstand crashed down, narrowly missing his skull; watched as Russo palmed off a sliding, chest-high filing cabinet that might have crushed a lesser man; and looked to the weapons cabinet.

Healey gave him a hopeful look.

Crouch nodded. "Rocket launchers," he said. "Time to step up our game a little."

Healey grinned like a boy with a new bike. Again he punched in the access code and pulled out the weapons. By now more of Crouch's team had made their way to his side. Crouch grunted as metallic pings clattered against the walls.

"Someone forgot to check our defense upgrade," he said. Which cast doubt on this being a Coyote operation; it was more likely to be a different, lesser enemy.

He felt the lurch as the shed slid out of their compound and onto the industrial park's streets. A slight turn and they were dragged over grass, through a briefly resisting fence, then they hit tarmac again. If Crouch had interpreted their movements correctly they were now traveling across the airfield.

Why? What on earth—

Then it hit him.

"Shit." He motioned for Healey to pass him one of the RPGs. "Best get a move on, lads. Unless you want to go for a swim in a tin box."

Quickly he checked and loaded his weapon, even as the jouncing shed jolted its way along the road. Another salvo of bullets ricocheted off the walls. Two of Crouch's men lost their balance and

17

rolled away as one metal edge slammed into the ground harder than before. An RPG slithered after them, worryingly already loaded. The shed travelled uphill for a short while and then hit a long downhill slope. Crouch felt a table slam into his back and pushed it aside. The dead and dying mercs all rolled toward the far wall, one of them still groaning but seemingly incapacitated.

There was no time left.

Crouch lifted the rocket launcher and balanced it over one shoulder; not an easy feat in the zigzagging shed. Healey did the same. Russo and the other men and women took cover as best they could. Then, with a shout, Crouch let the missile fly. The explosive warhead arrowed toward the shed-wall, fins spinning in flight. The downside to his plan happened next—the payload detonated on impact, sending metal fragments and fire bursting far and wide. Healey's missile hit further along, also detonating when it struck metal. A fireball mushroomed up the wall and spread across the roof, most of it escaping through the new ragged holes. Crouch, having prostrated himself in a hurry, looked up to see a torn-apart wall and scenery swishing past.

"Move it."

What was left of the Ninth Division struggled toward the blackened sides of the holes. As they approached, a new vehicle came into view; a flatbed truck, laden with men—their machine guns standing ready.

"Down!" Crouch yelled.

Bullets spattered the shed, peppering its frame and flying through the newly opened cavities. Fortunately the shots were all high. Crouch crawled hard, pistol in hand.

Healey was already there, firing through the gap at the swerving truck. When the shed gave another fishtail bounce it barely upset his aim; the bullet drawing sparks from the truck's rear tailgate. Crouch squinted and made every shot count, picking off one guy with a shot to the chest, making him tumble over the truck's low sides and smash to the ground.

Where the hell is the backup?

"We need to get out of here," he said suddenly.

For there, snaking along to the left, was the Thames itself, wide at this point and relatively deep, nothing standing between them and it except a half-mown flowery bank. Beyond the serpentine, reflective waterway, Crouch now saw lights in the sky, coming fast.

Helicopters. "Good guys are almost here," he said. Hoped.

He emptied the clip, forcing the truck to rev hard and surge out of sight after losing another soldier. Then he fixed Healey with a tough stare.

"Jump."

The young man blinked rapidly. Even his thirst for adventure was slaked a little by the prospect of jumping out of an office being towed by a bunch of gun-wielding mercs, it seemed.

"Stop being a little bitch," Russo growled. "And get your shrunken balls airborne."

The big man showed an example, leaping ungainly through the jagged gap, just missing a sharp curve of metal, and landing in a bouncing tangle of arms and legs on the bank outside.

"Now if you can't do better than that," Crouch said. "You're sacked. All of you."

Healey jumped. Crouch pulled up the next man. But, as his remaining half dozen soldiers lined up to escape, they all felt a sudden jerk and swerve in the motion of the shed. With abrupt savagery it swept to the left, almost as if the vehicle pulling it had swerved hard right.

And it had, Crouch realized. *This is where we hit the goddamn river.*

The shed suddenly tipped, the side with the holes slamming into the earth, then slithered dramatically down the steep slope. Crouch lost all sense of balance, tumbling head over heels and hitting the far wall. Debris crashed all around him. Bodies glanced off his legs; some screaming, one grunting deeply as bones audibly snapped. Then, as their minds became used to the speed of the slide, the shed's momentum was instantly arrested as it struck the water.

All quieted for a moment; then hell erupted.

Crouch had lost all sense of direction, not even sure which way was up or down. He struggled to his knees, noticing the swirling water already flooding the shed. A pile of papers floated by. A handgun knocked against his left arm as if reminding him it might yet be needed. He shook his head and tried to focus.

A hand gripped his right shoulder. "Sir! We should—"

The face disappeared as the shed shifted and a heavy filing cabinet rammed into the man. Crouch tried to help but the force of the collision tore him away and crushed him into the far wall. Before Crouch could do anything else the shed drifted sideways and sent its contents barreling in yet another direction.

Crouch saw the only way out of this thing was to head for the holes. He crawled as fast as he could, using the new floor to help him move forward. To hell with the torn nails, the lacerated fingers. The bubbling escape route was filling up fast with swirling debris and he needed to escape before it became too deadly. A deep, resonating groan echoed through the thinning air, bolts and welds already yielding to pressure. Crouch wasted no time. Nobody else was around him; he couldn't see a single person. So, unsure exactly how long he'd been dithering he simply dived into the big hole against the flow of water. Instant mayhem and confusion caused his heart to race. The surging current was strong, forcing him back. He flailed, kicking his legs. Another swirling flux spun him away and down, currents fighting each other as they tried to cope with the huge interloper. Crouch found his face hitting something soft, the river bank, and dug his fingers in hard. Already the breath was burning in his lungs, longing to be expelled. Desperate now, he forced his way up, using the bank to navigate. The surface was not too far, just a few feet . . .

White trails streaked through the water around him. Bullets!

But there were no choices left any more. Crouch had to keep on climbing, struggling. In seconds he would gulp water and die. The rippling surface was just feet away. A trail of fire ripped down his forearm, drawing swirls of blood. At last he broke the surface and gulped for air, momentarily unable to gauge his peril.

A splash sounded next to his ear. Any second he expected the lights to go out. But when he was able to open his eyes he saw a spectacular sight: Healey and Russo running and firing across the top of the river bank, tormenting the mercs that had abandoned their enormous tow vehicle and discarded grapples, and forcing those that remained to flee.

In seconds, Healey had reached Crouch and, still firing with one hand, reached down with the other to help him out of the river.

"You made them run?"

"Us," Healey said. "And them."

He pointed over Crouch's streaming shoulders.

He looked back, and saw two hovering choppers, packed with men. Crouch took another moment to look around.

"Where's everyone else?"

"I . . . I don't know, sir. You're the first we found. We thought we'd lost you too."

The enormity of their loss hit Crouch and he slumped. The Ninth Division had been decimated. Files and hard drives were replaceable. Men and women were not—particularly the group he had helped train and nurture during his reign.

Crouch felt fury infuse his body as he stared around at wreckage and death.

"Somebody's going to pay for this," he said. "And if it's all down to Coyote then that bitch is soon gonna wish she'd never been born."

CHAPTER THREE

Loss is the great identifier, the character builder, one of those times in life when one must prove one's mettle and struggle through. But there are many iterations of loss, many levels. Loss doesn't differentiate, doesn't take sides; it hits us when we're at our best or at our lowest ebb; and it takes no prisoners.

Matt Drake never got to say goodbye. Not to any of them. Alyson left their home in anger. Ben, Sam and Jo were murdered in the street. And Kennedy Moore —shot dead onboard a warship.

What did they all have in common?

The fact that they all expected to see each other again. The firm knowledge that, despite the anger and the miles apart, their last look had been one of friends that say "see you soon", not "goodbye forever". The fact niggled and messed with Drake's mind. He never got to say goodbye; never told most of them how he felt. And what about all that was left unsaid? Unknown?

Lost in time along with hearts, souls and minds that would never feel, never shine, never hold a loved one or a newborn child again.

On his way to the funeral in Leeds, Drake made a detour. He took Mai to the place where Alyson died.

With death playing such a major part in his life during the events in DC, and over the last year or so, it seemed right that, here, now, as they paid their respects to Ben and his family and were finally tracking down the enigma that was Coyote, that he visit the site where his wife and unborn child died more than eight years ago. The B-road was a meandering mess, replete with blind hills, curves and concealed exits from which tractors blasted out. More hazardous still were the steep and sudden drop-offs at either side of the road. No wonder the cops had ruled Alyson's death an accident.

When Drake reached the place, he pulled off the road and parked on the grass verge, front left tire partly in space. Mai had to clamber across the driver's seat to get out and join him at the edge of the road.

Drake stared down, eyes far away, oblivious to the fine English sleet that coated his head and shoulders. "They found the car on its roof. Eventually. Alyson . . . she died alone . . . in pain . . . knowing that her . . . her—"

Mai laid a hand on his shoulder. "Matt. This will not help you. We have been too close to death of late. It's like rubbing shoulders with the Reaper. Such exploits can only end one way."

Drake heard her words and immediately flashed onto her recent time in Tokyo. "What happened with you?"

"We will talk later."

He nodded absently. The sharp slope, he saw, led to a jagged pile of rocks and a small stand of trees. How had Coyote planned it? And *why?* If Coyote actually *was* Shelly Cohen, then they had been friends. They shared a mutual respect.

He was aware of what had happened to the Ninth Division. Thank God Crouch and some of his team had made it out. And to those that hadn't . . . he bowed his head again, thinking about how death and destruction could swamp you with its relentlessness.

Mai patted his arm. "We should go."

He took a last look, knowing that this was the last time he would ever visit this place. A raw sliver of hurt opened wider inside his gut. Not a sign remained. Not a single sign that Alyson and Emily had died here, alone. It shouldn't be this way. When a man's wife and unborn child died there should at least be some mark, some final sign or piece of evidence. It was all so—uncaring.

Drake turned away and strode back to the car. When Mai had settled herself he put the car in reverse and then stamped on the gas.

Worse was soon to come.

Drake found himself seated beside Karin, amidst a large crowd, on the afternoon of Ben Blake's funeral. Seeing so many people both angered and pleased Drake. In the end Ben had forged his own path. The members of his band were there. His girlfriend's grieving parents. Other college friends that Drake didn't know. Kids that shared the block of houses where he lived.

Mai, Alicia and Torsten Dahl stood on the fringes like dark-clad guardians, watching over it all. Komodo was seated to Karin's other side, a great hulking black-suited figure with a soldier's frame and tears in his eyes.

Drake fought his way through it, thinking a war would be easier than a fallen comrade's funeral. When the rituals were done and the formalities over, Karin turned to him with a look of utter despair in her eyes.

"We're here for you," Drake said, feeling simple and foolish. What were you supposed to say at a time like this?

"I feel like I might scream," Karin said.

I know the feeling, Drake wanted to say, but stopped himself. Karin had lost her brother and her parents in one day.

Instead he held her. The sleet coated them like a soothing balm and the commiserations of fellow mourners gradually faded away. The last fading vestiges of Ben Blake were lost, a firefly's last spark in the night.

Drake became aware of their surroundings again; the crowd melting away. Something was happening at a nearby hotel, a final farewell, but Ben's sister and the rest of the SPEAR team felt no compulsion to be there. The smell of a freshly dug grave stung Drake's nostrils. The low murmur of consolation rolled around his ears. When Mai, Alicia and Dahl joined them at the front he knew that he needed nothing more than this.

Karin clung to Komodo. "Let's get out of here."

Drake started to walk, his eyes barely raised. It was only when Alicia grunted in surprised disapproval that he looked up.

Half a dozen black cars were parked along the road that cut through the graveyard, effectively boxing their own in. As they watched, every door opened and tall, wide men in suits climbed out. Dozens of them. In their hands were clasped every numb weapon a savvy street-youth could imagine—from hammer shafts to stone-filled socks to baseball bats. Drake made himself blink twice before he allowed himself to believe what he was seeing.

"What is this?"

"Don't worry." Dahl put himself first in line. "I have this."

"But Torstyyy," Alicia mock-whined. "There are more than two dozen of them."

"Ohh, I'm scared now."

Alicia smiled and cracked her fingers. "This will actually provide a little light relief."

"Isn't that what they're here for?"

"Hope so."

"Wanna challenge? Best head-count wins."

"You're on."

As the gang approached, Dahl and Alicia opened out a gap in front. Mai glanced over at Drake to gauge his reaction. The Yorkshireman shrugged.

"Go for it."

Faced by a force more than seven times their size, the three-person phalanx waited to act. Komodo covered Karin who stared with utter disbelief; even now, after all that had happened, unable to consider this kind of event happening on the day of Ben's funeral. Behind her, several mourners were returning, good men and woman all, having seen what was taking place. Cellphones were already out and the more adventurous were stalking up to the front.

Drake watched as the group of men and youths ranged out and paused. Faces set, eyes hard, there was no doubt as to their intentions. Drake saw two further men heading for the car he'd arrived in.

But why blunt weapons? Why not the usual selection of guns and rocket launchers?

Before he had time to think, the attackers surged forward. Dahl smashed into the first three, scattering them end-over-end like bowling pins, then grabbed another by his long hair as the guy raced past. A high-pitched squeal and a blur of motion, then the guy was airborne, spinning and crashing into two more of his compatriots.

"Six!" Dahl yelled for good measure.

Four seconds had elapsed.

Alicia face-palmed her first two opponents, then kicked the third in the crotch. She didn't yell out because she was losing, but beckoned more attackers toward her.

"C'mon boys," she cried out. "Get yer nuts cracked here!"

As more veered toward her, Mai stepped into the gap, finishing off several attackers that still writhed around and another that had started to climb to his feet. Her face showed that she disapproved of both Dahl's and Alicia's tactics, but Drake knew that both of them were aware that Mai was mopping up at their backs.

Dahl stood like a concrete column, arm upraised as a baseball bat descended toward him. Unable to dodge, he withstood the impact, barely flinching as the bat shattered and broke apart on his great bulk. Its wielder then stared at the Swede in shock and awe, mouth hitting the floor only a split second before his forehead caved in.

Dahl moved on.

Drake caught a stray, at first disarming the youth that had outflanked Mai then gripping his throat as he lifted him off the ground.

"Ay up. What's appertaining 'ere then?"

The youth's eyes remained blank, not registering the question.

"Oh right. Y'see, once back in Yorkshire s'pose I just revert." Drake cleared his throat. "All right, wanker. What the hell's going on?"

He shook the youth for good measure. Amidst hacking and a flourishing purple hue, Drake's captive managed to squeeze out a few words. "She. Wants. You."

Unconsciousness took him. Drake discarded the limp body with disdain, suddenly more alert. He watched Alicia deflect a hammer shaft, then use it to nullify two men; saw Mai neutralize another three; and watched Dahl stride through the middle of it all, a hurricane of energy and force, unbending. Already he had reached the line of their adversaries' cars and was turning back into the fray. He was just in time to catch a man in the act of assaulting the Swede whilst his back was turned. Not surprisingly, that man soon found himself flying over the roof of a Range Rover Sport.

Alicia smashed knees and heads on her way to Dahl. Drake heard their little exchange over the screams of broken-limbed men.

"Twelve!"

"Eight. Dammit, Dahl, ya got lucky. One more time?"

Dahl inclined his head. "After you."

Alicia picked up a bat, clearly resorting to desperate measures, but Dahl had already caught a tardily swung pickaxe handle in the palm of his hand and wrenched it out of its owner's hand. The two darted forward again, leaving agony in their wake.

Mai turned to Drake with a raised eyebrow. "Always a pleasure going into battle with those two."

"Pleasure's all theirs," Drake grunted. Now that the immediate danger was over he scanned the perimeter before turning to Karin.

Ben's sister's face said it all. There were no words. Their world, their life, was never going to be normal anymore. One more crazy day like this could be just added to the mounting pile. Komodo, looking odd in his smart suit, nodded at the line of cars.

"Did see a few kids heading over to the cars."

Drake had seen them too. "Stick together," he said. "And let's go."

The four of them picked their way through Dahl and Alicia's chaotic battlefield, Drake having to administer two knockout blows in order to further subdue some of the more spirited opponents. He was careful not to completely incapacitate anyone, as Dahl and even Alicia had been. These youths had been sent poorly armed for a reason and Drake had no doubt they had no clue who they'd actually gone up against.

It would be a mysterious one for the memory-banks, if they retained any memory of it at all.

Drake and Mai scanned the row of cars, remaining vigilant as they cleared each opponent's vehicle. By the time they reached their own, Dahl and Alicia had rejoined them, both grinning and breathing easily.

"Great way to start the day," Alicia said instantly, before remembering where she was and throwing Karin a long-suffering look. The Englishwoman had confided very little since the events in

DC, but the Slayers had now departed to Europe for Lomas' and much of the rest of the gang's funerals. Alicia had chosen to remain with the SPEAR team, but Drake had the impression she was still running, still searching, refusing to lie down and grieve or take comfort—especially now that another she had clearly loved was dead.

Dahl, in the lead as ever, had stopped near one of their cars. After a moment's pause he fell to his stomach and checked the vehicle's underside, the wheel-wells and small cavities. As Drake approached he saw that something was stuck to the windshield.

"A parking ticket?" Karin wondered. "Surely not."

Drake stared. The object was a padded envelope, and it had four names typed in bold across its face.

"I guess I know what this is."

CHAPTER FOUR

Drake scooped up the envelope and exited the cemetery in a hurry. Nobody spoke again until the team were safely entrenched in a hastily booked hotel suite. It wasn't just that they didn't trust safe houses anymore, though understandably so, it was mostly because they could already guess some of the particulars and parameters that might exist within the contents of the envelope.

Once secure, Drake opened the envelope and upended its contents. A small, silver voice recorder fell out, clattering onto the table with a plastic rap. The team simply stared at him. Drake reached out and pressed the 'play' button.

"Hello, Matt." The sugary tones almost made him shiver. Old, great memories mixed with shocking betrayal and pure disbelief. Even now . . . even now he struggled to believe.

"And greetings to Torsten, Alicia and Mai, I hope. This message goes out to all of you. You are invited to attend the tournament of the decade. The world's best killers will be there, thirteen in total. You will have twenty four hours to become the Last Man Standing, to prove that you are the best. For you, Drake, it offers the chance to face me—Coyote, also known as Shelly Cohen in case you haven't recognized me." Laughter.

Drake gritted his teeth in silence.

"I will join the fray once ten hours has elapsed to spice up the battle. For Torsten, Alicia and Mai it offers fair competition and the chance to help your so-called *family*. But make no mistake, team—this is purely *last* man standing. Only one can walk away."

"But how—" Komodo stared to say, but Alicia waved him to silence.

"You may be wondering how I can hold you all to this? Well, if you don't turn up I will kill you and your families. I'm sure you know by now that I can do it. And it will be slow—and painful—dragged out for years." Coyote's sickly laughter hummed through the tinny speakers. "As for your other questions, know that our tournament takes place in the heart of a sleepy country town. I already have enough explosives inside the town and around the perimeter to wipe it off the face of the map. I'll reveal the location later but I warn you—tell no one. I will know. Exploding bumpkins are not your goal. Yes, I have other surprises, but it would be a shame if I revealed them all *before* we start, don't you think? Check the classifieds in the *Post* tonight, last edition. And do not disappoint me, Team SPEAR. The world wants to know who is best. Let's find out."

Drake let the recording play for a while longer. Nothing else was said. The Yorkshireman held his head in his hands. "Shelly?" he breathed. "I just keep thinking she's being framed. Or coerced."

Alicia grunted. "I knew Shelly too. Nice chick, if a little slutty. One thing I do know is that Coyote is a part of this tournament. We'll see her and break her, whoever she is."

Mai's mouth hung open. "Did you really just call someone *slutty?* You? And I thought I'd heard everything."

Drake's phone started ringing. "It's Crouch," he said. "Quiet."

The commander wasted no time with pleasantries. "Just got a special invite, Drake. To your tournament. Guess I'll be joining you."

Drake frowned. "Won't that just make her job harder?"

"Who knows? This Coyote's clearly the cleverest bastard we've come across. Fooled me for God knows how many years. All of us."

"I always had my doubts about her," Alicia said with arms crossed.

Drake snorted. "Give it a rest. Just because now you think she's a slut? Damn, Alicia, the only boss you never slept with was the President."

Alicia smirked. "Ya think? Don't be too sure."

The room quieted. Even Drake narrowed his eyes to see if she was joking. Crouch cleared his throat down the phone.

"I never slept with Myles. Is that good?"

"Well, it'll save you a few diseases," Mai said practically.

Drake turned back to the phone. "We'll see you there then, sir." He finished the call and stood up. "So. Let's find out when and where were going."

Dahl looked around the room. "Which one of us do you think will win?"

Drake held his gaze. "So long as we get Coyote I don't care."

"Good," Dahl said. "Since it's obviously going to be me."

CHAPTER FIVE

The Yorkshire Post impatiently yielded its prize, falling open to the classifieds the moment Drake threw it on the table. The ad glared out at them with blackest humor: SMALL COYOTE FOUND. RECENTLY RELOCATED. HATES WATER. WELL TRAVELED. RESPOND TO LMS BY 8PM FRIDAY. A landline number rounded it off.

Karin looked on as Mai googled the number on her mobile phone. Ordinarily, the tech-geek would be the first to break out the digital aid but her mind was a wreck, her sentience a ruin. Having survived Kovalenko's blood vengeance, she wanted nothing more than to grieve. The man at her arm was doing the best he could and she loved him for it. But she was washed out, devoid of compassion and motivation.

She heard Mai say that the STD code belonged to a single town, called Sunnyvale, only about a forty minute drive from Leeds. Whilst Mai looked up some local knowledge, Karin again zoned out.

The story of her past, and thus her lack of ambition, was a sad one; not something she relished looking back on at any time, but grief and tragedy had again brought those past events into sharp relief. When she was young, highly impressionable, and full of life she'd been out chasing around with her best friend, Rebecca Westing. 'Go burn off some energy, you two,' her mother had said to them. And they needed no more prompting than that. Out, over the fields, past the relic of an old playground trashed by youths and ignored by the local council, and eventually into town they had run, savoring their freedom. They'd reached their limits, the furthest their parents allowed them to wander, quickly, and thought about running back. But Karin saw something. She headed down a blind alley—a *ginnel* Becca had called it—where something had been discarded. It was a rusted ruin, a wreck, but to two young girls it was hours of nirvana. A swing set, swaying gently in the breeze; an open-armed death trap.

Karin had seen the danger at once, but fended the feeling away. Becca had jumped on first, trying out a few tentative swings and then her face lit up.

"It works!"

Karin claimed the seat beside her friend. Up they went, higher and higher, aiming to touch the sky with their heels, until one of Becca's chains snapped and she flew out of the seat at an awkward angle; not only hitting the nearby brick wall with her head but also the concrete floor.

Before Karin had even managed to stop her momentum, the blood was pooling.

But Becca was breathing, groaning, even trying to move. Karin was young but she knew what she had to do. She ran for help. She'd raced to the top of the alley, out into the street and screamed for help. And it was then that she'd learned about life. An old couple stared hard at her, this young flush-faced girl, their eyes hard with contempt. They thought she was playing some kind of prank. The businessman swished by with his phone to his ear, too busy to help. The taxi driver rode on by, spotting a distant fare. The man in the black saloon mouthed an obscenity as she almost stopped him making a green light.

And all the while her best friend died, bleeding out. And Karin, so young, felt an agony of helpless frustration that threatened to burst her heart. In the end a young, female student helped her, but Becca had died. Becca was dead and gone and the life she would lead, the hearts she would touch, and the dreams she would fulfil would now never know her.

Karin fell by the wayside, despite the great efforts of her parents and brother. They had tried until it almost killed them.

And now . . . what would she do without them?

After Becca's death, Karin had nurtured the loss and turned life away, choosing not to be involved. As heart-breaking as that was, she was still clever enough to turn out right, to ignore the worse things in life that can swamp and extinguish a lost soul.

Karin returned to the present as she heard Drake's request to contact the guys back in Washington DC. As Drake placed the call and opened up the speakerphone she listened with a little lift of hope as Hayden's voice came on the line.

"Hey guys. Is it raining?"

Dahl snorted. Drake laughed. "It doesn't *always* rain over here, you know."

"So it is then?"

"Yes."

"Knew it." Hayden laughed lightly, but stopped quickly. Her recovery was progressing slowly and she'd barely gotten past the wracking cough part yet. Karin imagined Kinimaka was sitting beside her and soon enough the Hawaiian's deep tones came across.

"We're only allowing her to speak for three minutes a day. So enjoy."

Again Hayden laughed and this time did degenerate into coughs. Karin heard Mano apologizing. Her own eyes flicked to Komodo and saw the gentle smile there. The soldier and the SPEAR team had taken her out of a decade-long fugue, only for all the happiness to be blasted apart in a single night of violence. But Komodo was still there. He was her anchor, her safe haven in the storm.

And still she could not bring herself to speak.

Kinimaka's voice returned. "We have a few things simmering over here. Nothing world shaking. My sister Kono is being looked after in Los Angeles by the FBI. I have to say this Agent Claire Collins seems an extremely capable Fed. It was her fast actions that saved Kono's life on the night of the Blood Vendetta. Only hers. Oh, and President Coburn is about to appoint a new Secretary of Defense—Robert Price."

Drake didn't know the name, nor did he care. "Remember, Mano, the vendetta is far from over. The Ninth Division was taken out—that's part of Kovalenko's revenge. So is this prissy tourney we're being forced to enter. Keep your loved ones safe. That includes all of you."

Kinimaka's voice lowered. "We're as safe as can be, guys. But safe houses ain't what they used to be."

Alicia grunted. "Don't we bloody well know it."

Karin watched as Alicia and then Dahl walked off to make their respective phone calls. The Swede's family—wife and two daughters—had recently arrived in DC. Karin had never seen Dahl worry before, but this was different. The man's heart and soul were gently held within that family, as fragile as spring flowers. Nowhere was safe. Then there was Alicia, who spoke at regular intervals to her biker friends. Especially Laid Back Lex, who wanted to join her. But Alicia would have none of them in her life at the moment; it was enough that she kept in contact with them.

Kinimaka continued to talk with a little help from Hayden. Karin flicked her eyes over to Mai when the Japanese woman's text message tone went off, and so did Drake. Was it Smyth? The hot-tempered soldier did like to keep in touch with his incarnation of perfection. Of course it could be Grace. Their young new addition was still being processed around the world and no doubt, like all teenagers, possessed the art of being able to text, eat and talk at the same time. Karin didn't possess that art, nor did she want to.

Mai texted somebody back. Kinimaka updated them on Yorgi and Lauren Fox. Both were still ready and eager to help if they could. Sarah Moxley was another matter. It would be some time before the reporter was able to help anyone.

Alicia slammed her phone shut and then, on hearing Mai's annoying text message alert once again, stomped over to the smaller woman and grabbed her phone.

"Really?" Mai asked with exasperation. "Are we school children now?"

Alicia wiggled her thumbs with surprising speed, reading aloud as she typed: "Sleeping with you would be like sleeping with one of the seven dwarves. And no, I'm not telling you which one. There. Send."

"No!" Mai yelped and lunged but missed as Alicia danced away.

"Don't worry. It'll at least keep him quiet for a while trying to figure 'em all out."

Drake made a point of ignoring them both completely, studying his speakerphone with huge interest. Karin had noticed a little distance between Drake and Mai since they returned from Zoya's place; nothing cumbersome, but Mai was definitely struggling with something.

One thing Karin knew for certain. It wasn't Smyth.

She listened hard as plans were made. She feared for their futures but couldn't see any part she could play. Perhaps it was for the best. For her the past had again caught up with the present, and the black hole it presented was already threatening to drag her down. Komodo was her anchor, sure, but who would secure him?

CHAPTER SIX

Tyler Webb surveyed the great kingdom a life of privilege afforded him. His grandfather and father had done all the work, netting billions. Once they'd died, Webb cast the everyday annoyances of running one of the world's biggest corporations aside, deferring them to well-prepped lackeys, and began the real work of his life.

The Pythians.

A child's dream perhaps, and indeed envisioned in childhood, Webb had always been fascinated by secret orders. By small shadowy houses purported to rule the world. When it became known in certain circles that the Shadow Elite were such a house, such a society, and had finally crumbled, Webb quickly put aside his incredulity on hearing that all his suspicions were true and considered how he might begin establishing his own.

A feat unknown in modern times. A new order with new rules, attempting to infiltrate and rule old, recognized circles. But it could be done. It could be done with money. Power. Influence. And, most important of all—with overwhelming, mortal fear.

His first act was to consider fellow members. Webb, an arms billionaire and leader in the field of nanotech, already knew several unscrupulous individuals. But he needed to stick to his parameters. Only those with unlimited power, influence and money could be invited to join. And for the Pythians, only the best, most lawless sinners in their field would be worthy.

So followed highly secret communiques to Miranda Le Brun, to Nicholas Bell of Sanstone Building, to General Bill Stone, to Clifford Bay-Dale and to Robert Norris—a man that actually sat on the board of SolDyn, the world's biggest company. Webb hadn't chosen these people at random. He'd spent weeks and months vetting them, gently exploring them, and then quietly testing them. At length he'd assessed them again and again, finally happy with his candidates and requesting an entirely covert, unidentified meeting.

After this came more tests and finally this day—the great day of their first true meeting. The new Pythians would sit together for the first time, and the new order would commence.

Webb had spared no expense; from the highly capable security team, the military grade surveillance and computer mainframe protocols, to the twenty-square-mile blanket suppression of all signals and monitoring of all nearby traffic, whether it be vehicle, airplane, or had two or four legs. With nothing left to chance, Webb was able to relax and even feel a little excitement as his guests began to arrive.

Webb sat at the head of a rectangular table. He wanted no illusion as to who was the principle partner in this particular collaboration.

"We are the Pythians," Webb said, once everyone was seated, sipping champagne and eating fish eggs and oysters. "Welcome." It was the opening line he intended to use at every meeting. "First order of business—news. What do we have?"

General Stone spoke up first. "With Kovalenko's demise and failure to test the nano-vests we've had to rethink. If those vests had gone off under DC and killed the President, we would have announced our shocking entrance to the world. As we stand we're now trialing them in the UK through Coyote, a master asset. Results should be in soon."

"Still," Webb said. "It leaves us without a 'grand entrance' into the game, don't you think?"

"Sure," Stone said. "Of course. There's always the 'house on the hill' scenario."

All the Pythians were well acquainted with current events and new group suggestions through an impregnable e-mail system.

"A bit extreme, Captain." Nicholas Bell, the builder and least liked of the six of them, saluted as he spoke. Bell was more than rough around the edges. He spoke as if he'd been dragged up, acted like a rough lout most of the time, and showed little respect for his fellow members. But Bell, with his worldwide construction network and endless resources, offered the group a tremendous amount of options. Webb believed the man would become more than invaluable.

But perhaps they could video-link to him in the future.

"Extreme," Stone agreed stoically. "But effective."

Webb held up a hand, a signal to table the subject for now. "Let's move on. Please keep us informed of the UK events, General. Now. Pandora?"

"The start of our great quest," Robert Norris, the SolDyn executive said. "Begins there. The plague pits are being sought by our forces across the world. Our one problem at the moment is a lack of manpower."

Webb nodded. Norris was the ultimate sneak, the man that had dirt on everyone. It would pay dividends to keep a close eye on that one. "We are recruiting as fast as we can. And don't forget, Pandora—though huge—is only our first foray. No need to rush."

"We believe there are three sites," Norris continued respectfully. "London is one. As I said we—"

"Yes, yes. We heard." Clifford Bay-Dale, the stuck-up prick that controlled more than half the world's energy, waved Norris's concerns away with a flick of his well-manicured hand. Recently, energy bosses had quickly become known as the world's new super villains, squeezing even more from the needy population despite humongous profits. Bay-Dale was by far the worst. In his mind, he deserved every penny; a privileged son-of-a-bitch that owned much and believed he most certainly should do. "Is there anything more interesting to speak of?"

"Only that you should all start vetting second and third degree memberships," Webb said. "Our sphere of influence should increase exponentially, and soon. It goes without saying that all second and third degree members will have no direct contact with the principle or first degree members. Use go-betweens. Miranda? Do you have any input?"

Miranda Le Brun, the sixth member of the Pythians and a bored oil heiress, simply shook her long hair from side to side. "No."

"Okay then. More manpower will be available soon. Pursue the Pandora angle to its limit. Prep the 'house on the hill' scenario, keeping in mind that any other scenario would be preferable at this point. We don't want to become known as mother-and-child killers."

"But if needs must." Bay-Dale spread his hands expressively, smugly.

"There comes a time." General Stone said firmly. "When the best man's boot should be stamped on the frail weakling's neck. With our inauguration, that time has arrived."

Webb gauged the feelings of his new order. All eyes were amenable to any possibility. *Good,* he thought. *It means I chose them wisely.*

The world was about to shudder in fear. It was about to be gripped and squeezed by the hand of the new Pythians as they sought to establish a devastating foothold. And more than that—the new rulers were coming and they were not benevolent masters.

Fear, Webb thought. *Fear is the master of the working class as well as the elite. We will own them all.*

CHAPTER SEVEN

Drake slid the rented 4x4 into a spare bay and looked dubiously at the rusting pay-and-display machines.

"Wonder if we should pay?"

"We're not tourists, Drake," Dahl said severely.

"I bloody well know that."

"Though by the way Drakey was driving," Alicia put in breezily, "you might think otherwise."

"Shut it," Drake said. "Haven't been behind the wheel for ages. Haven't had a good car chase for . . . months. Remember?"

"Yeah. The American freeway and airfield chase." Dahl smiled in fond memory. "Shelby Mustang ate you up that day."

"Bollocks," Drake said. "In any case, next time will be the decider."

"You're on. Once we sort out Coyote we'll book a track day. You, me and two Aston Martins."

"Wouldn't you prefer a Saab?"

"Can we stop talking about cars?" Mai spoke up. "And concentrate on the tiny problem at hand. You know—Coyote?"

Drake took another three-sixty perusal through the windows. "Well, this is Sunnyvale. Quiet town, which is good. Everything matches what we learned on Google Maps." They had memorized the town's layout prior to setting off and driven around it before parking. "Half an hour to kick off. We should get going."

"And dark already," Mai noted.

The team climbed out of their car, standing for a moment to take in the feel of the place. The setting was quiet, broken only by the occasional passing car or barking dog. No youths roamed the streets or lingered outside the local newsagents and takeaways. Roadways and streets were wide and obstacle free. Streetlamps were fully functional. One downside was that at least three different routes led to the castle, more to the train station. Stores and businesses closed early here, which the team counted as a plus. Market Street was built on a sharp incline, and contained the wrapped-up white hulks of many stalls. Alleys, dark narrow passageways and winding paths lay everywhere, havens for murderous assassins.

"This way." Dahl marched off. Drake and the women followed. The classified ad had provided a telephone number in addition to the STD code, the digits of which were actually coordinates. Dahl would now locate them on his preloaded mobile app and pinpoint their rendezvous area. A faint breeze whispered around the foursome, cool and carrying with it the mingled scents of hearth fires, cooked dinners and beer from a nearby pub. Sounds surrounded them too—the laughter of locals chatting across a garden fence, the trundling noise of someone maneuvering their wheelie bin up a paved path, the rapid passing of a man on a fast bicycle, the loud booming of a TV show behind drawn, bright curtains.

Dahl led them past a mid-size roundabout and along a route that led out of town, noting the small police station and fire station that nestled in next to each other along the way. Alicia examined them with a critical stare.

"Let's hope they're filled with red-blooded, meat-eating, rugby-playing village boys," she said. "I have a feeling we're gonna be needing 'em before the night's out."

Mai cackled. "Feeling a little horny, Taz?"

"Piss off."

Dahl walked past the edge of town, until flat fields and hedgerows filled the landscape. Out here the wind picked up several notches and lost a few degrees of warmth.

"I'm not lost," the Swede said as Drake opened his mouth. "As you know navigation is one of my many fortes."

Drake held up his hands. He could already see their destination, unlike Dahl who had his nose almost buried in the smart phone. In the end, he just pointed.

Dahl nodded. "Yeah, that's where I was headed next."

At the center of a nearby field, two dimly lit cabins stood amidst a chain-link fence with builders' wooden signs all around. It was a flippant disguise, but it would work for a night or two. Way beyond the paddock Drake saw a carnival outlined against the dark Ferris wheel and other rides slinging passengers around.

"I guess we know where most of the villagers went," he said.

Dahl took point again. Drake was under the impression that the Swede wanted this business over with quickly so he could get back to his family. *Twenty four hours,* Drake reasoned. It wasn't so long when you put it into perspective.

On the approach to the paddock's locked gates, Dahl slowed. Men melted out of the night, weapons raised. One of them approached.

"We've been waiting for you."

Drake shrugged. "We're here now."

"Follow me."

They were led through the gates and into a sparse cabin. A pockmarked wooden desk held papers and other contraptions that were being closely guarded. The man walked around the table.

"All right. Listen up. Last Man Standing is kill or be killed. Only one person can win. Got it?"

"We hear you," Mai said evenly.

"As for other competitors . . . there's Vincent, an undefeated assassin also known as The Ghost. Gretchen, a Russian special-forces killer. Blackbird—once of Mossad and their best. Need I say more? Duster, a Cockney lunatic. Santino, a nasty piece of work from Mexico City. Oh, and Gozu . . ." the hard-faced man cast a faintly amused glance toward Mai. "I'm told to tell you he's the clan's *second* Grand Master assassin. And finally, we have the best of the best. Possibly on level par with the Coyote herself, though never let her know I said that." The man winked. "We have the most notable French contract killer of all time—Beauregard Alain."

"Shit, you're kidding me." Alicia said. "I've heard of him."

Drake nodded. "That bell end escaped an entire SAS unit fifteen years ago. Killed two men in the process. Hope he's slowed down a bit."

"Believe me," their greeter assured them. "He hasn't." He handed out sheets of paper with facts, figures and mugshots attached. "Everyone has a set of these. Learn their faces well so you don't off any of these poor townsfolk tonight, eh? And by 'off' I mean—"

"We know what you mean," Dahl growled. "As if you care about these people one bit."

The man shrugged indifferently. "I get more money if this whole thing goes under the radar, that's all. Now, we have placed several . . ." he paused, ". . . preventative measures hidden around the town. Snipers. CCTV cameras. Mines." He coughed.

"*Mines?*" Mai exploded. "Are you crazy?"

"Raving fuckin' bonkers, lady. But that's part of my charm, and part of the deal. Don't try to leave or get a message out. We will know. Finish the goddamn tournament. That's why you're here. Now—on to the technical stuff."

The man pushed several items across the table toward them.

"Basic Bluetooth-equipped burner phones so we can get in touch with you. Take only the one with your name on it. Look often for text messages as well as listening for calls. Yep, it could get you killed in an awkward moment, but that's a risk I'm willing to take." Yellow teeth grinned sickeningly from between thin, cracked lips.

"This is a chip that will monitor your vital signs," the man went on. "Geoffrey here is going to implant you with it."

Drake stared at the small injector gun and its tiny dart. He shook his head. Alicia and Mai protested more vociferously and even Dahl looked uncomfortable.

"I didn't make the rules," the man said. "I just enforce them."

Alicia stalked around the desk. "Let me be clear, fuckhead. No prick's going inside me that I don't want there."

"No prick," the man said. "Just a jet of air."

"Not interested," Alicia said.

"All right." The man pushed across a tangle of straps and metal boxes. "Tie them tightly to yourselves. The signal will transmit through Bluetooth. If they come off it thinks you're dead, which means in relation to the tournament that you are dead. And you will be killed by any man—on sight. We can tell the difference between real death and the removal of the monitoring system."

"Much better," Alicia muttered.

"Guns?" The man sighed. "Let's see them."

Drake gave him an innocent look. "This is the UK. Guns are illegal."

Wands were passed over their bodies. When nothing bleeped or shrieked the man eyed them with a kind of amazed confusion. "You haven't brought any weapons?"

"Why?" Dahl rumbled. "You know who we are. Do you really think we need them?"

The man blinked hard. "Okay then. Onward. We're almost done here. For information we have a real army of men surrounding this town, folks. I can't warn you enough about trying to escape or get a message out. A late entrant, guy called Crouch who you know, might be a little late to the party. But he's a lucrative takedown. Almost—" the man eyed Drake. "As lucrative as you. Be warned. Beauregard Alain will care only about the big money." He indicated the final piece of equipment on the table, a chunky black box with a large screen. "Nope, it's not an ancient iPad, it's a location device."

"Shouldn't you be keeping that?" Alicia said in a droll tone.

"Not this one, love. It's a—" he made a face, "cheap bit of crap to be honest. It shows the locations of you and your erstwhile competitors. Only thing, our resident genius tech engineer," he nodded to a closed door, "has installed a very clever modification to the program. It refreshes not in real time but once every twelve minutes. You understand?"

Drake nodded. "Keeps it interesting."

"Doesn't it?" The man grinned. "Oh, and two final things."

"Is it the location of the food tent?" Alicia asked quickly. "I'm bloody starving here."

"The Coyote will enter the competition when ten hours have elapsed. *She* is the most lucrative target of all. Her choice. And an extra little challenge when she joins—she will reveal the locations of four special nano-vests attached to four citizens around the town. The vests will be wired to explode within a short time limit. The rest is up to you."

Drake regarded the man with hatred. "When this is done we *will* come for you."

"Well, at least somebody cares about the citizens," the man said. "All the other competitors just laughed."

"When do we start?"

"It's almost eight." The man referred to his watch. "Best get going."

CHAPTER EIGHT

Back outside, they were led beyond the dim cabin lights to another gate and showed through. Beyond that, dark fields led all the way to the outskirts of the carnival.

"Go through the carnival," a faceless soldier said, "and back into Sunnyvale. It's already eight o'clock. The game of assassins has already begun."

Alicia scouted the route ahead, taking off fast and staying low. It didn't take long to reach the carnival grounds and soon the four new contestants were walking along the wandering, muddy byways. Bright artificial light glared down at them from tall floodlights, and vivid neon splashes danced across their vision. Children ran without seeing, their small fists clutching bags of pink cotton candy and toffee apples. Queues formed around a huge bouncy slide and at a homemade curry stand.

Alicia eyed the slide. "Y'know, do we have time? I fancy a go on that."

Drake laughed and marveled silently about his oldest living friend's constitution. Inside, Alicia was a crumbling wreck. Outside, you would never know she'd seen a bad day in her life.

Dahl gave her an odd look. "I can never truly tell when you are serious."

Alicia was already on her way. Drake saw her eyeing the queue, the people in it, and the men and women that hung around its fringes, and knew there was more to her request than she was letting on. He threw an arm around her shoulders.

"What do you see?"

"I hate these fucking perverts." Alicia motioned toward more than one individual. "They stand around and they watch. It's their eyes that give them away. Too hungry. Too calculating. Always observing instead of being lost in the moment with your child. If I had kids . . . God, I could never let them out of my sight."

Drake hadn't heard this from her before. "Oh. Were you and Lomas . . . ?"

"Don't be a dick. No. I've always looked out for these perverts. Everywhere I go. Even been known to quietly neuter a few in my time." She smiled. "Literally."

Drake winced involuntarily. "Good job."

"It's Santino," Alicia said. "Right there."

Drake almost gawped but caught himself at the last moment. Alicia had clocked one of the assassins whilst scanning for pervs. He likened the man to the picture he'd recently studied. Santino was staring at mothers and children coming down the slide and, as Alicia said—his eyes betrayed him.

Dahl said with a touch of irony. "But we haven't even broken out the tracker yet."

"Okay," Drake snarled. "This is gonna be a real pleasure."

As one, the team melted away to Santino's blind side. Dahl checked behind the slide and gave Drake a thumbs up from pitch darkness. Mai moved to Santino's left, Alicia to his right. As a unit they hemmed him in without showing a single sign of hostility.

When they were ready and the slide was at its busiest with mothers, fathers and kids changing around and grabbing happily at each other, Alicia walked in front of Santino and gave him a sideways glace. With his attention grabbed, Mai struck hard and fast, smashing blows into his voice box, eardrum and ribs with three rapid blows. Then both women took the gargling, unsteady man under the arms and dragged him to the side. Drake followed, concealing their actions as best he could.

"Caught you in the act," Alicia hissed into his good ear as they laid him out behind the slide, rowdy generator booming alongside. "Your weakness betrayed you in the end, Santino."

The assassin bucked and struck out, catching Mai a glancing blow across the temple, too well-trained and dangerous to die without putting up a fight. He sat up fast, still choking, only to find Torsten Dahl's size twelve planted firmly in his face.

Santino collapsed again, skull cracking against the hard ground. Alicia watched as his face twisted in agony.

"Too good and fast an end for the likes of you," she said. "I wonder what else we could come up with."

But the man called Santino hadn't acquired the fearsome reputation that had earned him an invite to the world's greatest fighting tourney for nothing. The agony did not matter. The crushed bones did not matter. All that mattered was escaping, fighting now to reap vengeance another day. With a spine-twisting body flip he was up and on his feet in less than a second, whirling on Alicia soon after that. The startled woman fell back in alarm, narrowly missing the wide arc of a blade. Santino leapt through the gap she'd created, scrambling through the slippery mud back toward the carnival.

"Feisty bastard," Alicia said. "Should have made sure."

"Don't let him get among the people!" Dahl cried.

Drake took off after him like light chasing shadow. Mai was alongside, ranging to his right. Santino tripped and rolled under the air-filled slide, coming up in the darkness beneath. Drake dived right in after him, but the man's heels were as fleet as a scared rabbit's, carrying him fast to the other side. Drake was only inches away when Santino broke back out into the night and veered left, into the main body of the carnival itself.

Drake pursued hard, his eyes set on Santino as the assassin walked among families, long-bladed knife held flat along the side of his leg, not instantly noticeable but still poised to be used.

The group entered the carnival again, pushing through crowds and stopping errant children from getting too close to the assassin. The man paused once, at the back of a long queue at a donut stand, and fixed Drake's entire team with a black stare; the stare of a soulless man, a merciless killer. Children formed most of the line in front of him. Carefully, unobtrusively, he raised the knife and placed its tip at the bottom of a boy's spine. The warning was clear.

Drake stopped immediately, along with Dahl. Mai forced herself not to cry out a warning. Alicia was nowhere to be seen. Santino nodded and left the queue, twirling the knife on the tip of his finger. The only woman that noticed pulled her children closer, but laughed along with them as they watched, caution in her eyes.

Santino veered his ambling gait toward the carnival's exit.

If the assassin noticed Alicia was missing he gave no sign. In Drake's opinion the man must know she was AWOL. They had underestimated this assassin, and probably how good most of the participants were in this little charade. It would never happen again. Indeed, Drake wanted to live and tear apart the clouds that roiled between Mai and himself. And he wanted to unravel the many mysteries they'd discovered at Zoya's place. The Russian monster had hoarded myriad secrets. And he wanted to slide a dagger into Coyote's neck. For all these dreams to come to pass he had to survive this night.

Last man standing.

At any cost.

Now, he flicked his head at Mai. The Japanese ninja read his intent loud and clear. She melted into the crowd, flitting along its edges like silent, unseen death. Drake and Dahl increased their pace. Santino glanced back at them once more, eyes barely widening when he noticed what had happened.

Now the decision was his. Try to carry out his threat and die, or run to live. He chose the latter. He broke quickly for the exit, not anticipating the turnstiles. Though they were open they still clogged the path and the milling people did nothing but get in his way. After several moments of frustration Santino lost his temper and pounded toward a nearby collection of games and amusements stalls. Drake was well aware of the need for discretion. The last thing they needed now was a carnival brawl that brought cops from far and wide. He moved fast after Santino, then stopped in amazement as a carnival-ground basketball flew through the night and connected squarely with the assassin's face. Santino halted as if he'd run into a brick wall, blinking and dazed. The basketball bounced away amidst chimes of young-sounding laughter.

Alicia appeared from the middle of a crowd, spinning another ball on the tip of her finger.

Santino fixed her with a glare of hatred. He leapt at her, snarling, but again experienced only pure shock as he landed face-first in the dirt. Mai had stepped in from the side, tripping him before he even got started.

Drake and Dahl stepped in, hauling him up by the armpits and laughing at the nearby people. Drake imitated a man downing many pints as Dahl scooped up the discarded knife and tucked it away. Santino fought and struggled but the combined strength of the men holding him gave him little room to maneuver. Fathers laughed. Mothers looked stern. Even those working the stalls smiled.

Drake and Dahl manhandled Santino past the last stall and into the shadows that surrounded the fence around this place. Tall trees stood alongside and hung their high branches overhead. The lights and laughter seemed far away. As they turned Santino around and flung him up against the fence, a couple jumped up from the overgrown brush not far away, both in states of undress and fleeing with clothes unbuttoned and pants around their ankles. Alicia chortled after them.

"I'd put that away before I reached the carnival, little man."

Drake stood back from Santino, giving the assassin air. "We're fighting in a tournament that I intend to win, dickhead. So here's your chance. Go for it."

Santino didn't need to be told twice. Fast as a striking snake he struck at Drake; jab and punch, jab and sidestep, another knife appearing in his left hand, then more thrusts, feints and sharp punches. Drake ducked and dodged, letting Santino's blade tangle in the side of his jacket.

Santino wrenched it free. The heave unbalanced him.

Drake pounced, breaking down the assassin's defense in seconds and leaving him writhing on the ground. Blood coated the grass all around.

Dahl looked sideways at him. "*You* intend to win?"

Drake smashed Santino's face into the dirt with his boot heel. "Who else is there?"

Alicia and Mai were staring too, perhaps waiting for the punch line. Drake didn't have one and wasn't about to make one up. Not on this day. Not when Coyote was so close.

Santino gurgled. Drake started to pile brush over him. Mai finally hunkered down alongside him. "He's done. Let's move on to the town and finish what we came here to finish."

"Sure. I can do that."

Alicia kicked at the slow-moving mound. "This is actually better than he deserves."

A quick weapons search had found a utility knife, a military blade, and two powerful but small handguns. Drake handed the weapons out and consulted the map. Alicia swatted it aside.

"Let's just get away from this piece of dying shit," she said, "and worry about the damn town when we get there."

She walked off. Drake looked at Mai and Dahl, sharing a moment of startled bewilderment. One thing only was Alicia Myles' constant—she was never predictable. Numb to the visual delights and mouth-watering smells of the carnival, the four made their way through the crowds and the temporary stalls toward the heart of the town of Sunnyvale—their own personal Ground Zero.

It had begun.

CHAPTER NINE

Mano Kinimaka surveyed the new safe house, unable to shake the deep-rooted feeling that they weren't secure. It might have something to do with what had happened to most of the previous safe houses the big Hawaiian had stayed in; it might have something to do with the fact that Kovalenko had always found them—and they were still trying to shake off that damned Blood Vendetta. And it might have something to do with the woman he loved being so fragile, so vulnerable at the moment that his heart stilled every time she missed a beat, every time she coughed.

His nerves rattled like skeleton bones.

When Smyth burst into the room to inform them that all was okay with the world, Kinimaka almost drew his weapon and shot him. In his mind Smyth was immediately a new killer, a new threat. Then he recognized the man and let out a deep, heavy breath. *I need a break. We all do.*

For so long now they had been constantly fighting.

When the telephone rang he caught the movement of his hand just before it reached his shoulder holster. Not that the piece of inanimate plastic would have minded being shot to pieces, but the caller might.

Robert Price—the new Secretary of Defense.

"I wanted to touch base," the man said on speakerphone. "To tell you all that your country needs you, and that your country will wait for you. I do have plans, new plans, but I will not proceed without you."

Kinimaka, feeling clumsy as ever, reached for the phone before remembering it was on speaker. "Thank you, sir. We'll be ready."

"And the rest of the team?"

"They will return in a few days." Kinimaka said with a heavy heart. "Once the funeral is over."

"The British Ninth Division has been destroyed. Did you know that?"

"Yes, sir. I heard."

"A silly question, I imagine. Well, we'll talk soon."

The Secretary was gone, not even having asked about Hayden. Kinimaka stood up carefully and walked over to the window, staring down across DC. Their current safe house was at the very top of one of DC's tallest buildings, with as many as seven escape routes at their disposal. Smyth was acquainted with every one. Kinimaka should have been, but could only remember five—Hayden had started coughing toward the end of the briefing.

Now the dying afternoon sun washed across the Capitol, sparkling off the roofs of cars and the windows that lined the sides of buildings. From up here, you could imagine a world at peace down there; a companionable, compatible environment that was not at all fake.

Kinimaka knew better. The true monsters of this world kept their claws and terrible hungers hidden far away from the eyes and ears of real men. They struck from the shadows into the backs of their mightiest opponents. They used wicked, powerless cohorts to do their dirty work. They crouched unseen, laughing among themselves at their horrific achievements, craving the next one and the one after that.

His eyes swept DC, from the Capitol building to the Lincoln Memorial and further afield. Out there—monsters lay in wait. The world would never be safe and Kinimaka knew that a handful of heroes could never hope to keep up.

Hayden whispered his name. He turned to see her watching him, eyes as sharp as ever, a faint smile drifting around the edges of her mouth.

"Is Washington still safe?"

Kinimaka rolled his eyes a little. "For now."

"Spring is coming."

"And with it unsettled weather, I know."

"Business as usual then." Hayden's smile grew broader.

"Business as usual." Kinimaka crossed over to the bed and leaned in, planting a kiss on her forehead.

"Tell me what's happening, Mano."

The Hawaiian brought her up to date, knowing that Hayden thrived on new information and the act of moving forward. Becoming stagnant, she often told him, was what got you killed in the end, no matter who or what you were.

Hayden didn't look happy. "And this girl, Grace? How do we know she's not a damn assassin? A spy?"

Kinimaka shrugged. "That decision is on hold until Mai returns."

"I see. Is Mai in charge now?"

"No. Of course not," Kinimaka said. "I am . . . for now."

"Then *take* charge. Find out who Grace is and why she's here. If she's above board then at least we'll know."

Kinimaka nodded. "I'll have the Bureau step up the investigation."

"And Lauren Fox? Yorgi? They won't stay with us for long if we don't give them something to do, Mano. Get them involved. As for Sarah," Hayden closed her eyes briefly. "She should probably be allowed to drift away."

"As soon as the vendetta is finished."

"Which brings us full circle," Hayden said. "To this odd tournament Drake and the others have been called to. I guess there were threats and ultimatums issued by this Coyote or the team would have found another way. So how do they all intend to complete it and still survive?"

"They're our four best operatives," Kinimaka said unassumingly. "And not without help. Karin and Komodo are close. Michael Crouch of the Ninth Division is also involved and mightily pissed off. The contestants going up against them will be formidable, but if anyone can come out of a tournament called Last Man Standing with four living contestants it's Drake, Dahl, Alicia and Mai."

"Good point," Hayden conceded. "Is—"

At that moment, Smyth smashed through the door. Kinimaka stayed his hand as it reached rapidly for a weapon. But Smyth's quick words made the hand reach again and froze the blood in his veins.

"Mercenaries!" he shouted. "Or assassins. They're here now, coming fast. We need to get the hell out."

"How?" Kinimaka cried in frustration. "*How?*"

Hayden reached up from her hospital bed. "Doesn't matter," she said. "Could be any of dozens of runt infiltrators or a man like SaBo, the computer genius that helped Kovalenko attack DC. Could be a chance sighting. Smyth's whining heard through the walls. Text message tracing."

"All right, all right," Smyth snapped. "Stop yapping and start moving. Where to?"

"One of the seven escape routes." Kinimaka started to unstrap a few of Hayden's less important tubes.

"All compromised," Smyth said.

Kinimaka stared at him, fear threatening to engulf his chest. "What?"

"Every one gone. Dozens of men are coming, man. First four are about a minute away. What's your plan?"

Kinimaka looked around the room, fear for Hayden threatening to overwhelm his mind. "Draw weapons," he said.

"We can't make a stand," Smyth bit at him. "There're dozens of the bastards."

"I don't intend to," Kinimaka said and fired.

CHAPTER TEN

Drake hugged the uneven wall that formed the row of stores leading up a short, curving hill and onto Sunnyvale's main street. Every few feet another storefront protruded out, another hanging sign creaked, and another set of steps descended into the storage basements below the stores. Windows, though covered with hand-written signs and special offers, gave alternate views up the hill. Mai had been given the job of watching the rooftops, Dahl of watching the many winding alleyways that dissected the town, and Alicia of covering their rear. It was Drake's job to move them forward.

He hissed suddenly and the group crouched low, all with weapons raised. But it was only the shadow of a cloud scudding across the moon in a window three storefronts away; a miniscule movement but still one that required instant evaluation.

Darkness hung all around, painted by a master using darker hues in the most dangerous vantage points. And although the stores were closed and the carnival had attracted many townsfolk, the pubs were still noisy and frequented by many, the streets and side-streets echoed to occasional laughter and footfalls. Lone men and women walked by with their dogs; a man sat on a bench staring into space; a middle-aged couple played tonsil-hockey in a doorway, not even noticing the team pass close by them.

At the top of the hill a dark, narrow alley led away to the left up to an expansive graveyard and large church. The main road crested the hill then swooped down at a sharp angle, widening to create an impressive thoroughfare with stores to either side and market stalls all along the bottom. Little cafés with names like Frog Restaurant and Little Mo's and Penny's Coffee Bar revealed Sunnyvale's small-town nature as much as the tiny stores, community boards and handmade signs. Another sharp hill led off to the right toward the castle, Drake knew, with still more dissecting it.

Their opponents could be anywhere. They embraced the shadows for a time, letting their eyes wander and delve, and then begin all over again. The fact that it was still early and people still roamed the streets would not deter a master assassin. Collateral damage was a factor of their occupation, and one sometimes used to their advantage. So whilst Dahl was muttering about passers-by being so frivolous and devil-may-care, Mai was watching the shadows behind the passers-by and the ones that lurked ahead of them.

Dahl finally broke out the tracker. Its tiny flashing lights actually caused a potential security threat to the user, as they could be seen for yards around, but might also be useful.

Mai made a face. "Thing's pretty useless."

"Not entirely," Dahl disagreed. "We can fix their positions every twelve minutes and see if we can't figure out a pattern."

"And they'll be doing the same to us."

"Won't help 'em," Alicia pointed out. "I have no pattern."

"It is pretty useless," Drake said. "Every shift on that screen, every movement, can be second guessed to be a ruse or a threat. But hey, if you wanna feel important, Dahl, then go right ahead."

The Swede ignored him, taking stock of the flashing lights then turning the device off.

Drake spoke up again. "You think Coyote will make good on her threat? The nano-vest thing?"

"I do," Mai said. "She has never given us any reason to doubt her cruelty."

"We would be best served by thinning out the field before her arrival," Dahl said.

"Don't get ahead of yourself, Torst," Alicia said. "We need to find the crafty bastards first. Killing 'em will be a whole new ballgame."

Mai shrugged. "One of your favorite pastimes, I hear."

"Killing?"

"Ballgames."

"Fuckin' sprite. Focus. Y'know. Drake, your bitch sounds frustrated to me. You not performing regular enough to keep her tame?"

Mai's eyes flashed even in the dark. Drake held up a hand. "There."

It seemed their patience had paid off. A shadow slinked up the hill past a few doorways and passed out of sight, a shadow wearing all black and moving like a prowling panther.

"Move."

They crept forward. Mai cautioned them that it could still be a trap. Newly procured weapons ready, they inched ahead until an unlit sign stopped them. Painted white and in the form of an arrow it pointed to the left, down an alley to a flea market. Darkness pooled down there like the midnight waters that swept the Mariana Trench, but at the far end a wide glass door reflected distant light. The image it reflected was still, lifeless.

"Looks like a bloody trap," Drake said.

The faintest of scrapes echoed up the alley, something that could have been mortar crumbling, a crisp packet rustling, or a killer drawing a blade. Drake readied himself and hugged the near wall, taking Dahl with him. Mai and Alicia slinked along the other. Closer to the flea market's entrance they crept, passing a stockade of trash cans and a row of wall-mounted air-conditioner units.

Drake put his hand on the flea market door.

"Open," he said. "Someone's inside."

"We'd be stupid to follow," Alicia said.

"Agreed," Dahl whispered. "I believe we should—"

The door slammed into Drake as a figure hit it hard from the inside. The Yorkshireman stumbled back, surprised. A black-clad man squeezed through the gap and was suddenly among them; striking, punching, kicking with lightning speed, pushing his sudden advantage to the max. Drake stumbled beneath a flying kick. Dahl deflected a killing blow with a lucky uppercut. Mai reacted faster than even their assailant had imagined, stopping the blow that might well have fractured several of Alicia's ribs.

Alicia was gawping. *"Beauregard! Shit!"*

Drake jumped up. The Frenchman was unmasked, but also the only contestant apart from Coyote that might think he could take all four of them at once. Drake struck, but the assassin appeared to have some kind of sixth sense, evading blows from the side and behind, then using his opponents' surprise to his advantage.

Drake staggered, a knee having raised fire inside his right thigh muscle.

Alicia cried, "Watch him! He's as slippery and slimy as an oyster."

"Why, thank you," could be heard as Beauregard actually glided underneath Mai's offensive and came up kicking on the other side. Dahl lunged hard, but Beauregard unbalanced the Swede, spinning and sending him into a plastic trash can. Dahl's forehead connected hard, and left a great imprint and a huge crack. The mad Swede barely felt it.

Drake found his handgun at last, feeling that whole minutes had passed since Beauregard had started his assault but knowing it was mere seconds. "Stop," he said. "I don't want to have to shoot you."

Laughter crept all around him as the French assassin weaved and twisted from side to side. A black gloved hand knocked the gun to the floor. "Damn," Drake breathed, trying to keep track of the ghost.

"He's just smoke and shadow," Mai said. "Nothing more. One good strike will scatter him."

A gunshot rang out, loud in the alley. Dahl had drawn his own gun and fired at the darting shade. Drake heard the thunk as the bullet lodged in the wall at his back. In another second Beauregard had scurried high, using the trash cans and air-conditioner units to gain the roof in a matter of seconds.

"Jesus," Drake said. "That was close. Hope you measured that shot to the millimeter, Dahl."

The Swede grunted. "Worth the risk."

Drake gritted his teeth. "Everyone okay?"

"So that was Beauregard Alain," Mai said. "The stories may be true."

"What stories?"

"Really. You don't want to know. Maybe tomorrow."

"Well, that just fills me with confidence."

They exited the alley and moved back cautiously into faceless rows of storefronts. Mai tapped the folder they'd been given.

"We should get acquainted with the other assassins," she said. "Before we rush headlong into another fight. We need knowledge, a plan. We need to force *them* to react, not us."

Alicia pouted. "You mean we're gonna have to do some reading?"

Drake nodded, already reaching for the file. "Yeah. And fast."

Dahl leaned back against a wall. "So tell us about the people that accepted the offer, and would love to get rich by killing us tonight."

Vincent, The Ghost, was a contract killer that hired himself out to the highest bidder. Didn't matter if the person that had hired him was subsequently gazumped by the person he'd been hired to kill; Vincent went with the money, providing you could dish it up. More than one story existed of Vincent marching a target to some safety-deposit box, clearing it out and then fulfilling the hit, but on his original employer.

Total anonymity enabled him to do this. Vincent wasn't called The Ghost for nothing. His art was concealment; often the first you knew that The Ghost had been hired to kill you was when you heard the whisper of steel across your throat.

Next up was Gretchen, the Russian. An old picture of her showed a woman that might well be mistaken for a member of an Olympic weightlifting team; something that put Drake in mind of watching old Olympic Games, when Eastern Bloc teams used to proffer male and female line-ups that were almost interchangeable.

"That woman," Alicia said. "Will not be hard to recognize."

"Photo's ten years old," Drake said. "And if she's stopped using steroids she could look as handsome as . . . well . . . as Dahl by now."

"Shut it, Yorkshire twat."

Gretchen was ex-special forces, as most of these paid killers tended to be. Her specialty was close-up strangulation, asphyxiation, using her muscles to end a man's life. Like a boa constrictor, once Gretchen enclosed you in her grip, the game was lost.

Blackbird was Mossad, one of the most feared special-forces agencies in the world. Little was known of the Israeli agent; hence the description that they remained 'of Mossad'. The Israelis kept schtum on the subject, typically proffering no information. Male or female? Nobody knew.

"That person might be a little harder to spot," Alicia commented.

"Sharp as a razor," Mai said. "That's been used to trim a tree."

"I'll trim you if you don't be quiet."

"Uhh, promises, promises."

Dahl carried on his emotionless monotone. "Blackbird has been called a freelancer by some in the Israeli government. It says: 'Blackbird never fights alone'. Others—still reputable sources—say he only carries out hits sanctioned by his bosses. Which begs the question—why is Blackbird here?"

"We'll ask him later," Drake said. "Next."

Duster was a Cockney and a weapons expert. Everything from knives to high-explosives and advanced armaments filled his résumé like a comprehensive menu.

"Where the hell did she find these people?" Drake asked. "I never heard of any of them before."

"Coyote has run among them most of her life," Mai said. "In one form or another."

Gozu's name came up next, the second Grand Master assassin from Mai's village and quite possibly the only free member of Clan Tsugarai. Gozu would want to exact full vengeance for his clan's shame, money for himself, and walk away with Mai's head.

"This is his theater," Mai said. "It is what the masters trained for. Covert assassination among civilians. Slip in and slip away, a shadow in the twilight, an art learned over decades and through hard experience."

Gozu had been identified and placed on a watch list by Dai Hibiki, Mai's old police friend from Tokyo. The picture they had of him gave very little away, except that he looked almost identical to Gyuki, the Grand Master Mai had slain and her old teacher.

They skipped Santino.

Second to last on the list was Beauregard Alain, the French assassin, also known around the world as Lucifer. Deadly, pitiless, without restraint or remorse, Beauregard was revered in the same vaunted circles as Coyote.

"All I can say is, to get all these celebrities together the bloody reward must be fantastic," Alicia pointed out. "Why would they, and especially Beauregard and Coyote, want to fight each other just for this?"

Dahl sighed. "Kovalenko's fortune," he said. "Was vast. He funded this, remember? The vendetta fund goes to the last man standing . . . and it is one hundred million. More to the person that takes down Drake and Crouch."

Alicia coughed hard and eyed Drake. The Yorkshireman frowned. "Don't be silly."

Alicia narrowed her eyes. "I could put my kids through college with that kinda dosh."

"You don't *have* any kids."

"Sure I do. Just because they call themselves the Slayers and are aged twenty five to forty doesn't mean they're not family."

"Last on the list," Dahl said. "Is Michael Crouch. Wonder where he is?"

"He'll make contact," Drake said. "I'm not worried about that."

"So what's first?" Alicia stared across the dark town. "What's the plan?"

"Track them. Draw them out. End this." Drake said and then turned to the companions he was closest to. "And get on with our bloody lives."

Mai's emotionless stare did nothing to ease his fears.

CHAPTER ELEVEN

After Kinimaka fired his Glock he ducked reflexively as the window exploded outward. The evasive action was for when the wind, strong at this height, whipped some of the flying shards back in. Hayden covered her top half with a pillow. Smyth just stood and watched.

"What the—ow!"

Kinimaka crossed over to the shattered window. "We're not running, we're standing," he said, pressing a panic button. "Backup's on the way. We just have to hold for a few minutes. Smyth—" he pointed to the window. "Out."

"What?"

"You know what to do."

"Shit, yeah. Doesn't make me happy though."

Kinimaka held his tongue. The ex-Delta man wasn't exactly a ray of sunshine most days and had been spectacularly irritable since Romero died. Something they were all trying to help him through. The Hawaiian heard noises and rushed to the door.

Smyth headed for the window and a two-hundred-foot freefall.

Kinimaka saw four men running in single-file formation along a corridor that led to Hayden's room. Only one of the men startled him, a mountain of a man with a mongoose's face—all furry and twitching—several inches taller and wider than even Kinimaka himself. The Hawaiian suddenly knew what it was for someone to come up against him in battle.

Hope the bastard's as light on his feet as I am . . .

Kinimaka hit the door just before the team leader got there. A bullet flew through the gap, slamming past his nose. The door crashed into place, and he turned the lock. A figure collided against it from the other side. Now his attackers couldn't get to them through the bulletproof door.

A terrible memory swept through his mind just as Hayden said, "Mano. They might have the code."

He remembered with horror the first time he'd come up against Dmitry Kovalenko. An overwhelming force had crashed a safe house in Miami, and they had known the entry code.

"Override it!" Hayden cried. "Override it and shut it down!"

Kinimaka punched in the code just as the door clicked open. Without a moment's pause, the frame burst inward, men with severe crew cuts following close after. Kinimaka wrenched at the first one's shoulders, spinning him in place—much to his surprise—and forcing him back against the shattered frame. Splinters tore into the man's face, making him scream. The second stumbled over him. Kinimaka stomped on the man's spine as he landed on all fours, and fired into the first man's ribs, putting him down for good. The Hawaiian leapt aside as the second man, prone, twisted and fired at him. Bullets whickered through the thin air he had previously occupied. Kinimaka collided full-on with the third man, not on purpose but with characteristic clumsiness. The man flew away as if he'd been shot from a bungee rope, disappearing back down the corridor. Now it was mongoose-man's turn, and the enormous warrior was still trying to fit through the broken doorway.

Kinimaka stared, almost transfixed.

And heard the whisper as a trigger was pulled behind him . . .

No! The second man! He . . .

A gunshot erupted. Kinimaka had no chance to get out of the way. The bullet ripped into flesh, bursting the heart, but it was not his own. He dropped to his knees, landing hard and turned to see the second man holding a gun on him, unfired, and Hayden holding a gun *on the second man.*

Even from her hospital bed Hayden Jaye had saved his life. The second man collapsed, instantly dead.

Then, all was rushing, heaving manflesh as the outsize monster rammed him.

Smyth felt half-a-second's debilitating fear at the sheer, dizzy height then made himself suck it up. The window ledge ended where nothingness began. Far below, the distant street nestled, terrifyingly small. Smyth thought about how fear could only control you if you let it. Romero would have felt no fear out here. Romero would have eaten his misgivings alive. But Romero was dead, and all that was left of him out here were Smyth's best memories.

Smyth clung with one hand inside the outer wall as he stepped onto the narrow, slightly-curved ledge. That hand gripped with a Hulk's strength whilst the other quested along the outside wall for a firm handhold. Strong, erratic blasts of wind tugged at his hair, his clothes. All the world was silence except for the brief terrifying gusts, any one of which might suddenly hit gale force and pluck him off the ledge.

Smyth looked down. Stupid move. He did it again, irritably, angry at himself for being a fool and then angry that he was angry. He punished himself for being annoyed by doing it a third time, then remembered that Kinimaka was already fighting four men inside and Smyth was their only hope against the rest that were assuredly coming. Taking a breath he inched along the ledge, gripping the outer wall with steel-taloned fingertips where the mortar had crumbled away between blocks of stone. The grip was nothing more than a way of helping him balance; it could never hold him if one of his feet slipped. His right hand now held the edge of the window; still a firm, safe grip but one he would have to relinquish in order to move on.

Damn, the ledge looked wider when we came up with this plan.

With the balls of his feet balanced on the rolled top of the ledge, Smyth inched outside the tall building with nothing but fresh air and a long drop at his back. Little gusts of wind tugged at his body like playful imps. A shard of glass snagged in the sleeve of his jacket, tearing through and destabilizing him for a second. He had to concentrate hard in order to carefully unhook it. Sweat dripped from his brow. Someone fired a bullet inside. Smyth prayed to God his people were all right. Mai Kitano popped into his mind and he hurriedly put her aside. This was no time to lose focus.

Smyth shuffled sideways, painful inch by painful inch. A series of firm handholds didn't speed him up, but gave him more confidence.

In a matter of minutes he realized that the tips of his fingers were chilling rapidly, and being scraped bloody. He compartmentalized the pain and chose not to see them.

Finally he reached the next room's window and reached out for the frame. Smyth never knew where he made the mistake; possible over-eagerness, a momentary lack of judgment and spatial-awareness, or the weakening grip in his hands—but his fingers missed the edge of the frame by millimeters and closed over nothing.

Unbalanced, committed, Smyth wavered.

And fell.

Kinimaka pushed hard against the man-mountain, the two men like dueling rhinos trying to throw each other to the ground. A meaty paw lay across his shoulders, pushing down on them with all the force of an industrial crusher, forcing the breath out of Kinimaka's lungs and making his eyes pop. The Hawaiian pushed back with all his might, but the monster had the advantage and was bringing his extra weight to bear. Grunting filled the air between them. Hayden couldn't fire because Mano was between the giant and her.

Kinimaka saw the man's other hand coming around. In it was clasped a big Magnum, reduced to the size of a toy pea-shooter in the veiny flesh and stubby fingers. Seconds passed that felt like minutes. The gun moved slowly, but inexorably, the barrel turning. As it lined up with Kinimaka's knees he half expected a fast bullet, but the giant was going for the kill shot. More seconds passed. Then, as Kinimaka saw the stubby fingers contract around the trigger, he allowed the giant's weight to topple him, unbalancing the man and making his ear-splitting shot pass harmlessly overhead.

Both leviathans crashed to the floor. Kinimaka recovered first, grabbed the legs of one of the dead attackers and swung the body around at the giant's head. The body actually lifted off the floor, shifting at speed, the shoulders crashing into an enormous chest and producing a satisfying grunt of pain.

But Kinimaka didn't stop there. He was in the fight of his life and knew it. He rose fast, swinging the inert body again, this time letting go at the last second and hoping the extra momentum would topple his opponent.

He stared in amazement as the monster stared and then simply swatted the dead merc's body from the air, just slapping it down like an annoying insect. It crashed to the floor, bones breaking.

"Mac never beaten." The growl was the sound of an approaching subway train. "Not start with you, little man."

Kinimaka blinked. In all his life nobody had ever called him "little man". Now he cringed as Mac stamped on the other merc's body for good effect, snapping whatever intact bones the man had left.

Hayden's voice snapped him out of it. "Get out of the damn way!"

Kinimaka just wasn't that quick. He was trained, he was fleet of foot, but he wasn't exactly Jet Li, for God's sake. Mac lumbered toward him, closing the distance fast. Kinimaka, out of time, met the giant head on. Their chests crunched. Mac's huge arms tried to wrap around but Kinimaka delivered four fast kidney punches that actually slowed his opponent. Kinimaka finished with an uppercut, his big fist connecting solidly with the other's jaw.

Mac's eyes closed and his body slithered to the floor.

"Thank God," Hayden said.

Kinimaka frowned. "I don't think he's—"

Mac rolled backward and tried to stand. When his knees wobbled he decided to stay kneeling, then grabbed hold of the side of the room's double sofa and hurled it. Kinimaka had nowhere to go. The sofa caught his lower body, sending him over the top and tumbling past the cushions onto the floor beyond. Mac was already there, looming above the Hawaiian.

"Nice try."

A shot rang out. Instant surprise creased Mac's eyes. The bullet flew above his head, but the frozen moment gave Kinimaka a chance. The Hawaiian scrambled away, hands and feet scrabbling amidst the debris, looking for anything that could give him an edge in this uneven battle of Goliaths.

A chair. Kinimaka picked it up, spun, and swung downward all in one easy move. Mac rose into it, forehead upraised, and the wood simply splintered and disintegrated all around him. Three long shards stuck out of the bridge of his nose, monstrous spines acquired in combat.

"Is that it?" Mac grunted.

"Stop!" Hayden screamed. "Stop, or I *will* kill you!"

Mac guffawed. Kinimaka was up against a wall. Mac charged and Hayden fired, the bullet punching into the enormous merc's side and lodging there. To the bullet's credit it did make Mac grimace, it made his body kink, but it didn't slow him. He hit Kinimaka head on, foreheads colliding with a heavy crunch. The wall exploded around them, plaster and timber and a single block wall smashed to pieces. Debris rained down and cascaded away. Mac fell on top of the Hawaiian.

Kinimaka blacked out.

Smyth windmilled his arms as he fell, searching for any kind of purchase. The one thing that could have saved him, the ledge, slipped smoothly across his flying fingertips, offering no salvation. Almost in slow-motion, he felt his feet falling through fresh air, felt the tipping of his body as his top half started to over-balance. Sheer panic ignited every nerve ending. The sudden pounding of his heart was so loud it felt like a heavy-metal drummer had climbed inside his head.

Not the best way to die, goddamn it.

Smyth flailed again, sensing another floor flashing by and that his increasing momentum meant this was his last chance. The ledge hit his hand, his fingers closed.

And slipped off!

Smyth screamed. Adrenalin smashed through him. Somehow, he bought a second chance; his fingers again closing around the ledge. By luck and good fortune his feet caught on one of the building's aesthetic outcroppings, a protruding figure-eight design of bespoke blocks. Even then his momentum was enough to make his feet slip and his fingers almost break.

But he held on. Panting, shaking, face pressed into the rough brick, he held on. And looked up at the window, just above the ledge. Panic wanted to take control, but Smyth wouldn't let it. He was a soldier, trained, honed. His friends were fighting for their lives. Mai hadn't texted him back.

With so much to live for and debts to dead friends that still remained unpaid, Smyth reached out and hauled his body up through the turbulent air. He gained the ledge, used his weapon to smash the window, and hurled himself inside.

A second was all he allowed himself. Then, body purged of excess adrenalin, he calculated his floor and ran headlong for the lifts. As a reward for his bravery the car stopped at almost every floor on its way up, but soon Smyth was inside and heading back up to the top floor; praying he wasn't too late; resisting the urge to check his messages. When the buzzer dinged, Smyth leveled his weapon and eased out into the corridor. The door to Hayden's room lay on the floor, the frame busted open. Bodies lay all around.

Mercs were filing toward the open door; new groups that had infiltrated the hospital using different means. At least eight . . . nine . . . ten.

Smyth didn't stand on ceremony. Without a word, he opened fire.

Kinimaka was unconscious. Mac was victorious. All the meaty colossus had to do was neutralize him. Instead, the merc chose to punch the Hawaiian's face into a pulp and it was the constant, painful blows that actually brought Mano back to consciousness.

Shit, that hurts!

Kinimaka opened his eyes. Another blow crunched into his cheekbone. Mac was above him; eyes feral, lips split and bloody, spikes of wood still sticking out of his face. The great fist he raised blocked out everything else, like a deadly, hard-hitting eclipse. When it descended at speed, Kinimaka lowered his forehead, still receiving a dose of sickening pain but also dishing out more than a satisfying measure. Mac yelped.

Gunfire sounded through the half-demolished wall that led back to Hayden's room.

Kinimaka firmed his resolve. This piece of shit might well be of tyrannosaur proportions, but it was still a piece of shit. He blocked the next blow with upraised arms then dodged the next, rolling to the side. Though his head still spun he managed to grab one of the cracked walling blocks and swing it in Mac's direction.

Mac's fist smashed into the lightweight block, breaking it apart. Another yelp issued from the beast. Kinimaka threw another and another, knowing Mac was too big to evade them. Next, he hefted a broken piece of two-by-four and swung that over and over at his assailant's head, making the man duck and cover. The wood landed time and again on exposed knuckles and wrists, flaying skin and drawing blood.

"Guess what, Mac?" an exhausted Kinimaka said. "You're about to lose for the first and last time."

The same thought had obviously struck Mac too. He withstood two more blows then charged forward, yelling, a lumbering titan with no concept of how to lose. Kinimaka inched to the right, rumbling loudly with effort and still thwacking his opponent.

Mac ran harder.

Seeing only one chance, Kinimaka slipped to the side as Mac ran at him, then, gripping his opponents armored vest, he hurled the man even faster on his course, the power of his arms practically sending Mac airborne.

And straight into the room's only window. Glass shattered, a thunderous fragmented explosion. Mac lurched to a stop half-inside, half-outside the window, bent at the waist. Kinimaka felt every urge to topple him over and out into the night, but couldn't bring himself to do that. Instead, noting the sudden lack of movement and hearing the drip of blood, he left Mac alone and ran back toward Hayden's room. Walls spun around him, his feet felt like they were inside flippers running across a pitching deck. His recently pounded face bones ached.

Ducking through the gap, he took blocks and timber with him, making the hole even larger. Back inside Hayden's room the first thing he saw was her grateful eyes, her shaking hands lining up a Glock, and then mercenaries flying through the door to her room.

Only they weren't running. They were stumbling, sprawling, collapsing in death spasms. Kinimaka stopped for a second, but one of the downed men began to move, prompting him to stomp over and put an end to such audacity. The Hawaiian stamped among them, dealing out punches and kicks and ensuring the wounded stayed down. At last Smyth put his head through the door, checking the scene.

Hayden breathed heavily. "Thank God. Now let's get our asses out of here."

But Smyth was staring over Kinimaka's shoulder with growing horror. "What the hell is that?"

The Hawaiian whirled, already fearing the answer. Sure enough, Mac stood there, but he was a terrible, twisted version of the nightmare figure that had already beaten and bruised him. The crag-like visage was bleeding, lacerated flesh hanging loose. The jaw was broken, twisted to an uneven angle. Teeth were smashed. The three spines of wood had been driven even further into the bridge of his nose and now protruded like small, deadly horns.

"Oh shit."

The monster charged, bellowing like resounding thunder. Death and hatred shone from those violence-crazed eyes. Smyth opened fire, pumping bullet after bullet into the oncoming mountain of flesh. Hayden fired too, emptying her Glock. At first the bullets had no effect but little by little they took their toll, slowing Mac down until he shambled to a bloody, heaving halt, right in front of Kinimaka.

The Hawaiian punched him square on the nose. Mac wavered, but he had experienced nothing yet. Kinimaka bent over as Mac fell, hefted the man's weight over his shoulders, and then lifted his bulk into the air.

Mac bleated, never guessing such indignity existed.

Kinimaka staggered under the weight, but tensed and flexed every muscle before throwing Mac across the room. Airborne, Mac pinwheeled helplessly, arms flapping like a mad marionette's. Gravity didn't give him much of a flight, but when it brought him back down to earth it did so brutally. Mac thudded into the floor with a sound that made all three of them cringe. The walls shook. The room seemed to sway, but that could have been Kinimaka's unsteadiness.

"Really?" Smyth stared around the room. "You spent all that time with that guy? What were you doing? The waltz?"

"Not now." Kinimaka hurt in a thousand places.

"You wanna know what *I've* been through?"

"No."

"Really? Well, I'll tell you anyway. First, I scraped my friggin' fingers raw on that—"

Kinimaka tuned him out as he scooped Hayden up and tried to figure out which exit might be clear and what they should do next. If safe houses were no longer safe, where could they possibly go next?

Somehow, the CIA houses in DC were fully compromised. *Only two places we can go,* he thought. *One, the White House, is closed to us. The other . . . might not be.*

A call to Robert Price should do the trick.

CHAPTER TWELVE

Drake led the way back down the steep hill. With no clear way forward, the team had decided to scope out the town's highpoints, reasoning that such intimate knowledge would come in handy later. The big church and its surrounding graveyard offered many places of concealment, but flushed out no assassins. Now, they were on their way to the train station and after that the castle. As a team, they weren't afraid of being ambushed; they were confident in each other's abilities to predict and react.

"Hey," Alicia breathed down the line. "Wouldn't it be easier to just go to the pub? You know, wait until all these assholes kill each other and then just take out the final man."

"Possibly," Dahl said with a big grin. "But where's the fun in that?"

"My guess is, Coyote's got something planned," Drake said uneasily. "They've mined the damn town, for God's sake. She has men guarding its outskirts. I'm betting her exit strategy will not be people-friendly."

"We need to avoid that," Dahl agreed.

"So we take Coyote out of the running as quickly as possible. Her plans will die with her."

They passed the flapping huddle that constituted the town's market. At the bottom of the street a road intersected, running both ways. The train station lay around the gently curving corner and across the road, swathed in darkness. A high dirty brick wall enclosed it, protected at its apex by barbed-wire mesh. The only way inside that Drake could see was a wrought-iron gate topped by spikes and chained with a padlock.

"Station's closed," he said.

Dahl waved the tracking device. "One blip has been stationed inside there for the past half hour. We don't know if that means they're dead, in hiding or something else."

"What about the three blips up at the castle?" Alicia said. "Another group?"

Drake shrugged. "We're here now. As much as I hate the idea of a tracking device that refreshes every twelve minutes, the question has to be asked—how else are we going to find them?"

The group kept to the shadows as much as they could, crossing the road and reaching the high wall that enclosed the station. Drake tested the padlock that secured the gate. "Locked," he breathed.

Dahl pointed up. "Over we go."

With a leg up the Swede was soon poised with his arms over the top of the wall, his eyes scanning the inside of the station. The top of the wall was just a little higher than anyone could boost him, so he had to remain still using only his arm muscles. After a few minutes he called down.

"It's quiet. I don't like it, but there's some cover right inside." He lifted himself over the wall. Drake gave Mai a leg up then waited until her arms reached back down toward him. Within seconds they'd crossed over the wall and were crouched in the shadow of a shed on the other side.

"We have to assume the assassin knows where we are," Drake whispered. "It's not exactly Swedish Special Forces we're dealing with here."

Dahl shook his head. "No. They'd have snapped your scrawny neck by now."

"Shh," Mai hissed. "Please. We have to take this seriously. Gozu is one of the assassins and even with Coyote and Beauregard involved I find it hard to believe there is anyone better."

Drake nodded in silence, accepting the rebuke. Carefully, he raised his head, scanning ahead. Their shelter lay at one end of the station, the actual terminus of the track. The platform led away on both sides of the rusty tracks, sloping upward. A ticket booth and store stood to the right-hand side and a low bridge toward the end of the platform. So many dark places filled his vision that he could barely tell them apart.

Between the shed and the next place of shelter, the store, lay about twenty feet of exposed ground.

"Hope Alicia's found a way in," he muttered. "This way couldn't be more dangerous."

As if in answer, a shout rose up from the darkness. Drake saw two quick things – a shadow approach fast from the far end of the platform and then another chunk of darkness shift amidst the deep shadows that clung to the roof of the store.

Alicia had caught someone's attention, and that person had moved, betraying themselves.

"Down!" Drake yelled, breaking cover. Instantly, the shadow above the store rolled again and a flash of light erupted. Drake dived for cover. A blast rocketed overhead.

"Was that a shotgun?" Mai gasped. She yanked on Drake's legs, pulling him back as a second explosion occurred about the same time a rocket of flame erupted from the path where his head had been.

"Almost blew my bloody brains out!" Drake twisted back into the shelter.

Dahl chuckled. "Not even an assassin's that good a shot."

Mai rose and fired one of the handguns, giving the assassin reason to doubt. Sure enough, knowing they'd been spotted, Drake saw the shadow flit off the edge of the roof and land, catlike, on two feet, poised on the platform.

"Again," he said.

Mai rose and fired. The shotgun spat flame. A throaty chuckle drifted through the air.

"It is Drake and his comrades, dah? Lucky for me. I fuck you up early and take prize." More laughter and an increase in gunshots as the assassin closed the gap.

Drake's mouth was a thin line. "Another fucking Russian. I've had my fill of fucking Russians lately."

"Must be Gretchen," Dahl said.

Mai peered out at a low angle. "Wait. Just wait," she said. "You know my thoughts on Russian-made items. Well, that's a Russian Saiga boomstick if I'm not mistaken." She held up five fingers and then counted down.

"Four . . . fi—"

There came the unmistakable sound of a gun jamming. Mai rolled instantly, firing hard. Drake and Dahl both broke cover, running up the side of the platform. As they sighted the Russian they noted Alicia advancing from behind.

Gretchen dropped the shotgun and whipped out a compact Uzi. Drake had expected all kinds of weapons present tonight—assassins knew how to smuggle their weapon of choice into any country—and so far he was not disappointed. Gretchen herself was on the large side, a slab of pure nondescript muscle from the Soviet era that could have belonged to either gender. No expression crossed her bland features. Her arms and legs were trunks of pure muscle.

When Alicia hit her from behind, the Englishwoman appeared to bounce off, her face twisted into an almost comical expression of shock. Gretchen merely blinked and brought the Uzi to bear, but then hesitated, as if unsure which direction to attend to first.

Alicia shook her head and rose. Drake and Dahl closed the gap rapidly. Mai's rolling gunshots passed close to the Russian but were too random to be accurate, especially as Mai had the added problem of also avoiding Alicia. But by now most of the team were converging on the Russian and the time for gunplay was over.

Gretchen saw it, drawing a wicked blade over twelve inches long. It was the first time any emotion touched her eyes—wicked and excited expectation. A pale tongue flicked across her lips.

"I gut swine like you for my breakfast."

Drake didn't doubt it. He paced warily outside the woman's swing. She may be big, muscle-bound and clumsy looking, but she certainly wasn't slow, this Russian travesty of times past. He studied as she adjusted to Dahl's movements and his own, and then to Alicia's padding up behind.

The problem wasn't taking her down. It was taking her down and remaining fully intact. The night was yet young and full of terrors. Even the slightest mistake could cost them the tournament and their lives.

With every sense and nerve on edge, Drake feinted. Gretchen ignored him, sensing it was a ruse. Instead she turned to Dahl.

"You are fine Englishman, dah? Big. Solid. We could make strong Russian babies, you and I."

Dahl didn't answer, but the expression in his eyes showed he knew he would take a few hits for that comment later. Drake feinted again, and again Gretchen didn't respond. Instead she whirled her deadly blade in an arc, almost catching Alicia as she moved in.

"Back off, little ferret."

Alicia held up both hands. "Already there."

Drake heard Mai moving behind him. Judging by the swiftness of her footfalls and the sharp flicker of Gretchen's gaze, the Japanese woman was moving fast. This was it, then. Mai had called the play. Gretchen couldn't help but track Mai, the approaching whirlwind. Drake and Dahl moved in. The Russian did the only thing she could; tried to break for it in Alicia's direction.

But as she moved, as she geared up that locomotive of a body, something fell onto her from the darkness that filled the train station's arched roof. It was a heavy shadow, a cloaked arcane thing. The first indication Drake had that it was human was when Gretchen's face opened up from hairline to chin, blood pouring out. The expression of shock in her eyes continued, the flicker and dart of surprise, even as she collapsed. She was still breathing when her head hit the floor, alive because her body hadn't yet realized she was dead.

Mai gasped into the silence, "*Gozu!*"

All hell broke loose. The Tsugarai's new master assassin moved like a dervish, flicking a shuriken in Alicia's direction, a small blade toward Dahl, and slicing the wicked sword he'd bloodied on Gretchen at Drake.

The Yorkshireman backpedalled, not expecting such a sudden onslaught. Within seconds the manner of the fight had changed. Gozu was like a spinning devil, the opposite of Gretchen, and the shock of his silent arrival had stunned them all.

Gozu leapt through the gap between Drake and Dahl, bursting toward Mai.

"Dishonorable bitch!" He spat. "You kill your master! Enslave your clan! You will pay in eternity for all that."

He struck like a thunderbolt; hands, feet and elbows stabbing forward faster than even Mai could track. Not only that, when one of his hands wasn't engaged in combat he filled it with a shuriken or a small blade, throwing the object at Alicia, Drake and Dahl, and even Mai. Drake found a knife sticking out of his shoulder that he hadn't even seen being thrown. Alicia cursed.

Mai struggled to defend herself, driven backwards, throwing her own arms and legs up in the nick of time but still taking hard blows to the face and ribs. Gozu was a killing machine, bred for a single purpose, and even Mai didn't possess the lifelong discipline it would take to stop him.

"And Gyuki!" Gozu spat. "My teacher and yours. You would murder him too!"

Mai double-stepped to the side, perilously close to the edge of the platform, but gaining valuable inches. "Gyuki was a child molester, a devil. He deserved more than the quick death I gave him."

Gozu raged, "I will—"

His tirade ended as Dahl smashed into him. Gozu's little distraction, as he listened to Mai condemn his master, had enabled the mad Swede to launch a risky onslaught. The assassin staggered back with Dahl wrapped around his waist. Almost any other man in the world would have folded, but Gozu possessed such strength and balance that he managed to stay on his feet, striking down onto the nape of Dahl's exposed neck.

The Swede grunted, coming up and letting go. Instantly, his cheek burned as Gozu whipped stiffened fingers across it. Dahl caught the second strike that would have crushed his windpipe, but missed the third that slammed into his gut and doubled him over. The Swede couldn't remember when he'd been hit so painfully, so accurately, the blow slamming directly into nerve clusters.

His brain filled with agony. It was all he could feel, see, and think about.

Drake was by his side. The Englishman engaged Gozu without pause, trying to limit the master assassin's strikes to the better protected parts of his body. Once he'd accepted that Gozu was inevitably going to break his defense at some point, it was a little easier to subtly direct those strikes toward less crucial areas. The two men fought their way back up the platform toward the store and a waiting Alicia.

"Tricky little fucker," she said. "Try this."

She flung her knife, giving Drake flashbacks of when she'd flung it once before, saving all their lives, but the Tsugarai assassin was more than ready for her move. With an eye-flicker of disdain he withdrew his short sword and deflected it away. Alicia cursed and joined the fight. Drake turned the directionality of the fight so that Gozu was headed backwards toward the far end of the station.

Right now the assassin was as far away from Mai as Drake could possibly get him. As they fought harder, Gozu hit the bottom step of the stairs that led up to the bridge that crossed the track and continued up, climbing backwards. Drake tried to take the advantage, increasing his attacks, but Gozu only twisted faster and punched harder. In the end, being a true Yorkshireman born and bred, the only thing Drake could think of was to be blunt. He picked up a man-sized sign with a solid plastic base and hurled it at Gozu's head.

The assassin slithered underneath, but lost his footing. The sign bounced back and hit him in the spine. Alicia delivered a stunning, twisting elbow to the nose, breaking it with a loud snap. If Gozu even noticed the blow he gave no hint, but scrambled on arms and legs up the stairs like an escaping insect. Drake pursued fast. By the time he, Alicia and now Dahl reached the Ninja, the man had gained the narrow bridge across the tracks.

"Running out of space, arsehole?" Alicia taunted.

But then Gozu showed his intention. His goal was Mai, and Drake knew it; and should have anticipated the next move. Gozu leapt on to the paint-flecked railing that spanned the bridge and simply launched himself into space. He landed lightly on the platform below and tumbled, then sprinted hard at Mai with a terrible, driven, singular purpose evident in every quick realignment of his body.

Mai faced him; calm, poised, as if expecting this charge all along.

Drake raced for the stairs, Alicia at his heels. Dahl, in his special way, followed the ninja-trained assassin right off the railing, landing heavy and with a loud bellow, but still managing to tuck and roll. He came up aching, shocked, but still in one piece.

By that time Gozu was firing everything in his arsenal at Mai. The Japanese ex-ninja skilfully stood her ground, retaliating when she could and dealing several severe blows of her own. Gozu was definitely deteriorating now, having held four world-class assailants off for so long and taking wounds along the way.

"Gyuki would have been proud of you," Mai said. "Such a loyal little worm."

"I *am* loyal to my masters!"

"And you will die loyal." Mai had purposely sought to raise Gozu's heckles, knowing that besmirching his clan opened up the only crack in his armor. When the man stopped for one split second and reacted with hatred, she darted in close and grabbed the short sword that was hidden among the folds of his black robe. With a deft tug she wrenched it partly free of its scabbard and sawed the exposed blade across his ribs. This time Gozu yelled out and half-folded. Mai danced clear. Gozu struck out blindly.

Drake pounded along the platform, closing fast on Dahl. Alicia raced past them all, so fast Drake gawped and so close he heard the mantra she repeated under her breath.

". . . will *not* lose another, will *not* lose another—"

Mai drove a foot into Gozu's knee, watched him fold more acutely, then stepped in to finish the job.

"No!" Alicia cried.

Only Mai kept going. She didn't see the small blade held behind Gozu's back, who knew that even in defeat he could still kill his enemy.

"I beat you," Mai said, leaning down.

Drake almost screamed. Damn, this wasn't like Mai. The Japanese woman usually dispatched her enemies with no real emotion, clinical to the end. One man down and move on to the next and the next until all enemies lay motionless and cold. But this battle was personal, so personal she'd allowed its meaning to scramble her senses.

Gozu rose up, destined to die but determined to extract his vengeance. The knife swung around, a mere distraction, and Mai fell for it. She turned and blocked the blade, leaving her neck open to Gozu's brutal attack.

He struck ruthlessly.

A band of unbreakable iron encircled her throat. Mai lost the ability to breathe, both her hands instantly coming up to try and loosen the crushing grip. This left her exposed to the blade.

Choking to death, she barely noticed. The blade plunged.

At the last instant, Alicia threw herself headlong at the pair. She crashed into them like a wrecking ball, demolishing the deadly embrace. The blade flicked away. Alicia tumbled on past, leaving Mai and Gozu prostrate in her wake. By then Drake and Dahl were almost on top of the ninja. Dahl bunched his huge fist into his robe and hauled him to his feet; Drake delivered a flurry of blows to his chest and midriff. The ones that landed on his open wound made him scream.

Drake didn't stop. Dahl held him and Drake punched him until he slumped, unmoving. After that Dahl threw the body onto the tracks, out of sight. The four of them regrouped at the gate that exited the station and caught their breaths whilst Dahl broke out his tracker.

"All right," he said after a while. "Their blips have stopped flashing and turned into stationary red dots, and so has Santino's, so I guess we can safely conclude this means no vital signs. Three down," he grunted. "Four bad guys to go. Not including *us*, of course, and Crouch and Coyote."

"What time is it?" Drake asked.

Mai looked up at him. "Time I bought you a watch."

"It's midnight," a disembodied voice told them and they all suddenly fell into defensive stances.

All except Drake. He knew that voice anywhere. "Michael Crouch, sir," he said. "I wondered when you would show up."

"Less of the 'sir'," Crouch said. "I guess I'm pretty much the civilian now."

Drake met his eyes. "The Ninth Division . . . I'm sorry. What of the people that survived with you?"

"Awaiting my call. And who supports you?"

Drake looked a little sheepish and glanced at his colleagues. "Communications are disallowed. They have civilians wired to nanovests, an army of mercs, some kind of computer genius and land mines." He shrugged.

Crouch gave him raised eyebrows. "And more I assume. But even in that short list there is something you can exploit."

Drake ran through it again in his head. Of course there was. But they would need outside help to do it, and from someone he didn't believe was operationally fit. Still, needs must. He opened his mouth to speak.

"Wait," Dahl said suddenly. "What the hell's that noise?"

He knew of course. They all knew. As one, their five faces turned white, hard and desperate.

"God help them," Mai whispered.

CHAPTER THIRTEEN

Thirteen, Coyote thought. *Unlucky for me, as always. I killed my first man at age thirteen. I am the thirteenth contestant.* She'd found out later that her thirteenth kill had involved the death of an unborn child. *If I were in a goddamn book, I'd be on chapter bloody thirteen.*

Coyote had known only one overwhelming urge her entire life—the need to kill. When it first came, the feeling initially consumed her, engulfing her until she could hardly concentrate on anything else. But she guessed from the very beginning that sloppiness would lead to exposure and discovery, and ultimately to death. At first her attempts to blunt her urges were infinitesimal—small animals—but it did the trick. What she didn't anticipate was that her disease would mature as she did, growing more complex and more demanding.

Eventually the animals were no longer enough.

Coyote was intelligent; a hard-working, likeable, sociable girl. The two sides to her were pure Jekyll and Hyde, one always lurking and demanding tribute whilst the other struggled to be the good girl everyone always thought she was.

As she grew she took martial arts and boxing classes, quickly demonstrating her ability to learn fast. The aggressive nature of the classes, five days a week, helped dull her urges, but only for a short while. The dark side didn't like it when she had to rein in her terrible impulses so as not to visit them upon the rest of her class. It made her pay by growing stronger.

Coyote knew all along that she was a psychopath. She'd migrated toward the Army because it offered the chance of fieldwork and missions, and the naïve young woman in her saw a chance to hide her urges in plain sight. Before she joined the Army she had killed, but the hard code that she lived by enabled her to disguise the body and get away with it. The man she'd chosen, a wife-beating gang-leader, was barely missed and barely investigated but murder was still murder, and taking a life was robbing a person of the chance to do some good.

After the Army took her it actually got harder. The scrutiny was strict, relentless. It was only when Crouch offered her the post at the Ninth Division, having seen her past exploits, that she found a little space in which to fulfil her base desires.

Coyote thought back now. Those times had been the best: so simple, so invigorating. She could travel alone and meet her mark in Paris, stay the night and take her time over scratching an itch with a very sharp knife, and then return to London with a clear head, ready to help her friend and mentor, Crouch, and the boys in the field to the best of her quickly developing abilities.

"Stay frisky," she used to say to help focus their minds on the job at hand and what waited for them back home, in *their* homes.

The 'boys' responded to her, most in a respectful, appreciative way, understanding her motives. The ones that didn't erred only once, and were taught the errors of their ways. All but one then got the idea, and the one that didn't was kicked out of the Army by Michael Crouch. Her boss, whom she respected completely, appreciated intelligence, initiative and skill but brooked no slackers. He was the very essence of the best boss an employee could ever have—one who had been where they were and seen everything that happened at every single level, not some shiny-arse rich man's over-educated son handed a leadership on the back of a club membership, a helpful vote or even a month's stay in some millionaire's holiday castle on an exposed crag of an Icelandic mountain.

Coyote became the world's greatest assassin by pure chance. A target bargained for his life; a real target, offering money, power and further jobs if she promised to take out his annoying partner. Coyote liked the idea. It gave her the chance of an extra kill, or at least pooling both jobs into one. It gave her a second supply line. It offered diversity, giving her the chance to use up stored vacation days. She informed Crouch that she'd turned the target instead of eliminating him, an action that actually brought her a promotion, and then started to take jobs, using him as an intermediary. After a while she grew wary of him, knowing she needed to preserve her anonymity or eventually lose everything, and spent a pleasant evening planning his accidental death. As her reputation grew he became less pliable and more dangerous, seemingly lacking the intellect to imagine he might become one of her victims. Later, she actioned her plan then set up a totally secure line of contact, three times removed from herself, through the dark Internet, a source even the US government were having difficulty penetrating. It could be accessed through secure, unhackable software exclusively available only to those that were allowed to purchase it. She used only the contacts she'd personally vetted and who knew how deadly she was.

Coyote never failed. She achieved the luxury of being able to quote her own timetable, her own methods. Unusually for one in her profession, she was highly trusted to close the deal.

At that point she could have lived her life out in happiness, killing those she was assured deserved it, building a legendary reputation, and even enjoying her secondary life as part of a superb team. The only downside was constantly pulling the wool over Crouch's eyes, and she took no pleasure in that.

Then came Commander Wells and his blind servitude to the Shadow Elite and the eventual order to stop Matt Drake from getting too close to the faceless sect of world leaders.

Coyote knew it was Wells that had unknowingly contacted her, despite his attempts at anonymity. The irony was laughable. But the dilemma it posed to her purported humanity, her friendship with the soldiers of the Ninth Division, and the hit her reputation as an assassin might take if she refused ran deeper than all the blood she had spilled. She resolved to take a slight hit, and pay Alyson, Drake's wife, a little visit, but not a fatal one.

That night, it had been raining. The roads were slick. Coyote saw that both the target and Drake himself were at home, a little fact that was not a part of her Intel. She considered pulling the plug, coming back another day. This was not part of the release for her, it would not be a kill. Alyson was one of her soldiers' wives. She could not be badly hurt. Coyote considered every option. In the end she figured that infiltrating the house was out of the question. Drake was a good soldier and would have installed security if not some kind of warning system and escape route. She determined to disable Alyson's car, reasoning that it was late and the couple wouldn't be venturing out again tonight.

Unlucky thirteen.

Driving away, satisfied that Alyson's accident would be only that and not a death, she'd fought to assuage the disquiet inside her. The job had requested a murder. But Alyson Drake was different. The job, her urges, did not require blind acceptance, and the innocent wife of a good soldier was out of the question.

Coyote had felt the rental car's tires slip a little as she rounded a tight bend and focused her attentions on leaving the area without wasting her insurance deposit.

It was hours later, as the news of Alyson Drake's death filtered through the system, that Drake's friend, Shelly Cohen, learned of the terrible accident and the two innocent lives it had taken.

CHAPTER FOURTEEN

Coyote scanned the monitors as she reminisced. The past was a minefield, fraught with mistakes and littered with broken threads that should be left well alone; scattered strands that led to the discovery of monsters, and she had learned to bury it as efficiently as a fresh kill . . . and yet—shards remained.

Shaking that off, Coyote acknowledged her computer genius, SaBo or Salami Bob, as he pointed to a monitor filled with colorful graphics.

"Signal went out there, about five minutes ago. I've been crushing these signals all night, monitoring the harmless calls, but the gunfire over at the train station produced a huge spike. Something went out." He turned to her. "The cops will respond."

Coyote drew a breath, standing to her full six feet. With long black hair, a well-defined face, and what appeared to be a curvy frame, she was often mistaken for a soft touch. There was a time when she'd enjoyed teaching people the errors of their ways. These days, she merely killed them.

Coyote had become disillusioned through time. If the old urges hadn't still controlled her desires, albeit with lesser frequency and insistence now, she would have already resolved to just fade away. Rock stars and movie stars did it best; they shone like comets for a short while and then faded right out, and you were always left wondering what had happened to them.

But Coyote could have done it too.

"We knew this would happen," SaBo said. "We never had a hope of smothering every signal and landline."

Coyote said nothing, merely waving her second-in-command over. "The cop station," she said. "Do it now."

"And the fire station?" he asked with a grin and a Southern twang. "They're dead on beside each other."

"I know." Coyote silenced him with a stare. But the man's query made sense. Better to silence both local emergency services at the same time. "Do it."

SaBo tapped a CCTV screen. "I see some other local responders," he said. "Possibly off-duty cops responding to the call."

Coyote didn't hesitate. "That's it then. Put the main plan into action. Destroy the local cell towers and put a cordon on all incoming roads. Send our eyes and ears out everywhere. Activate the escape plan. We're fully invested now, gentlemen. Hope you're ready for it."

SaBo looked a bit green. Her second favored her with his brightest grin yet.

"Locked in tight," he said, and strode away. Coyote watched him go, wondering if she would have to kill him later, and then turned her attention to the screen.

"Watch what happens . . ." SaBo used one of the high-definition monitors to zoom in on the police station.

The Sunnyvale police station was a small two-story building, relatively innocuous, that sat behind a flat, wide parking area. Trees grew close to its back and sides. The windows were wide, some of them sporting the newest law-enforcement slogans. Figures could be seen passing by the brightly lit frontage on both levels. Squad cars sat outside, ready to go.

The first thing the police knew about the assault was when two missiles smashed through the windows and exploded inside the building, one at ground level and one on the first floor. A third was fired, but detonated against the outer wall, its shooter receiving a death glare from his captain for his inadequacy. The RPG attack had been timed to occur seconds before a mercenary team assaulted the building, spreading quickly inside to corner their prey, to overcome them through sheer violent intent and force, and prevent any communications from reaching the outside. The mercenary leader had also found this kind of initial brutal attack often led to fewer casualties.

Of course all this was merely minimization, not prevention. Nobody on earth could stop this news getting out. But the Coyote only needed nineteen more hours.

The mercs wounded where they had to and locked up those that surrendered. The flames that licked around the offices were soon extinguished. The communications room was destroyed, though nobody could tell if a secret alarm had been tripped or some other method of silent contact had been utilized by the officers during the assault. The mercenaries took down the police and fire stations in less than half an hour, but it was fair to say the town's authorities had never seen the like of this before. Salvos of gunfire ripped walls apart, brought ceilings down, smashed windows and even squad cars outside. Broad, ruthless, well-protected men smashed skulls and faces, brooking no debate. The closest a cop came to real injury was when two mercs chose to dangle him out of a window in retaliation for throwing a punch, but then those mercs were reprimanded by their leader who was heard to say, "Not yet."

Local responders, en route to the station or the source of the emergency call itself were captured or shot down, depending on manpower. SaBo did his best to show Coyote every altercation and his best was very good.

"The only trouble we'll have now will be from the residents that live near those two stations," SaBo said. He pointed to the wrecked buildings, the clear cries that were slowly dying down, the groups of mercs still running rampant through the parking areas.

"For now," Coyote said. "In this kind of situation, trouble starts to escalate and, like a tidal wave, it will only stop when it crushes us into the ground."

"I'll try not to be here for that," SaBo said, coughing. "Can't swim."

"You're here until I say otherwise," Coyote said. "But fear not, I don't intend to sacrifice you. I've always considered mercenaries expendable, not computer geeks."

SaBo bowed down.

Coyote turned her attention back to the tournament. "What's happening now?"

CHAPTER FIFTEEN

Drake turned to the others.

"It's nothing but a show of force, I guess. They're subduing the local authorities, letting this tournament play out as much as possible. Twenty four hours is rather ambitious, but they don't even need that. Still, we do need help." His eyes fixed on Crouch.

"I already explained who you need. The single element controlling this entire area is surveillance monitoring."

Drake nodded. "Karin would have to take on Coyote's geek, head to head, and she'd have to win. To do that, she'd have to be at the top of her game." He shook his head.

Mai held up a hand. "She can do it. Give her the chance to step up."

Drake didn't have to explain what Karin Blake had lost recently.

"Well, one thing's for sure," Alicia said into the silence. "We four can't go. We're tagged."

Crouch chewed his lip. "I could get beyond the net, make the call, and return."

"Wait." Drake eyed him properly for the first time. "You're not tagged?"

Crouch almost smiled. "There's a reason I became leader of the Ninth Division, Drake." He tapped his skull. "Smarts."

"Coyote and her goons don't know you're here?"

Crouch nodded. "The only reason I didn't bring the British Army is because I knew Coyote would have set her tripwires and traps. I wanted to test the lie of the land first."

"Of course. Are you still as well connected as I remember?"

Crouch betrayed no emotion. "All the way to the top, my friend."

Drake knew the leader of the British Army's most successful covert operation's team wasn't referring to the Prime Minister. His influences ran a little higher, to the places where clouds obscured most people's view. He reeled off contact numbers for Karin and

Komodo and, as a precaution, for the remainder of the team back in DC.

"Karin should still be in Leeds," he said. "Do you have a facility with a rait good computer?"

Crouch raised an eyebrow. "*Rait* good? I realize we're in your home county, Drake, but less of the lingo."

Drake smiled a little, still unsure how to address his old boss of bosses. The situation was both awkward and a little delicate. Deep down, Drake was and always would be a soldier and Crouch was his superior. But now, not only was Drake a civilian, but so was Crouch. For the moment at least.

Alicia had no such qualms. "Okay, so the Crouchster hits up Karin, gets her on the job, and we carry on offing the bad guys. Sounds like a plan to me. What are you all waiting for?"

Michael Crouch moved away at pace. Alone, he ran the plan through his mind once again, reaffirming just how important the success of this particular mission was. Lives depended on him reaching Karin Blake, both civilian and military. He was aware of the girl's recent losses, but knew enough about her involvement in the SPEAR team's exploits that he trusted her to step up to the task at hand.

Crouch stuck to the back alleys, a detailed plan of Sunnyvale lodged in his mind. The destruction of the Ninth Division still stunned him, making even everyday decisions that much harder and causing him to doubt himself for the first time in decades. The field of action was just what he needed.

Toward the end of the alley a merc awaited. Crouch hugged the shadows, scanning the ground for debris that might give him away if he stood on it, and moving only when the motion would not be seen. He stayed low, outside the merc's natural line of sight. As he crept closer he saw the bored look on the man's face, the weapon cradled low, the Bluetooth headset flashing at his right ear.

It might be useful to commandeer one of the comms.

Not for long, he reasoned. Coyote and her captain would have some kind of protocol worked out. But even five minutes might yield some precious information. Crouch considered the man in front of him. He'd heard the saying: Mercs don't get old; and, in his way, had instantly understood every nuance of it. Mercs had no country, no home, no people back home that depended on them. This made their cause infinitely weaker. A soldier could bite back on his true origin when times got tough, whilst a merc? What could he bite back on?

A roll of bank notes.

Truth was, Crouch reflected, mercs rarely grew old enough to retire.

He darted forward, tackling the man's gun-toting arm first, bending it around his back until he heard the snap. With a whirl he managed to stick out a fist and stifle his victim's scream whilst at the same time bending his other wrist until it broke. Crouch finished with a savage strike to the forehead, using the man's own gun, and crouched low, testing the air.

Nothing moved. A television blared through a partly open upstairs window. A cat rustled by. Crouch took the weapon and the Bluetooth earpiece and proceeded across a main road then down the side of a closed supermarket. The two-minute dash put him briefly in the open, but it was still the safest way to the fields beyond the town. As Crouch reached the rear of the supermarket he paused, catching the smell of smoke drifting on the wind.

He listened, senses attuned.

Though he couldn't hear them or see them, he certainly smelled and discerned their nasty little habit. It had given them away. Plumes of smoke belched from a dark corner, among the supermarket's recycling bins. Crouch wondered if the men had been stationed there or were taking a spontaneous break. Either way, it mattered not. If he wanted to continue at pace he'd have to get rid of them.

He tapped the earpiece, muttered several garbled words and then said clearly, ". . . moving away from the supermarket . . . help."

Questions came back. Crouch ignored them. If the mercs had any discipline whatsoever they would check out the communication, possibly assuming one of their number was either compromised or under attack. The men back at their field office would need answers. Crouch waited. Within seconds the invisible men behind the recycling bins melted out of the shadows and proceeded boldly across the rear parking area and into the street. They looked both ways. Nothing stirred.

Except for Crouch, who crept among shadows, trying hard to keep his own discipline and not make an example of these shoddy men. A dozen far better than they had been gunned down during the attack on the Division. A dozen that he'd personally handpicked and trained, men and women that were just, fair and skilled, proud to be at their posts. Their losses could never be recouped.

It hurt Crouch deep inside. The pain felt as if the marrow was being stripped from his bones; a pure physical agony. It made him stop at the edge of the first field; it made him sink to his knees. Did he blame himself?

Of course. Shelly Cohen had set out to make a fool of him, and she'd succeeded. In fact, she'd succeeded so well that she'd destroyed his whole organization. Most of all, she'd succeeded so well he already knew that he was out of the British Armed Forces and their security games the moment the first bullet had been fired.

Burdened and bent, he nevertheless laid his own yoke aside and rose to the task. The field was dark, and led to one even darker. A number of land mines had been hinted at, but Crouch knew it was fair to say that if such an atrocity were true, they'd have been laid closer to main egress roads and points of strategic entry.

He wasn't looking for a road or an escape route. He was looking for a signal.

Another field and a high hedge stood in his way. The final field was heavily rutted and smelled of recently turned earth. At last, after twenty minutes of scrambling, the signal flashed up strong on his cell display. He'd reached the edge of Coyote's net.

Crouch tapped in Karin Blake's number, listening to the beeps as the call tried to connect. The night was cool out here, exposed to the scathing winds; the vast patchwork skies arching above like the roof of some great gladiator dome. The silence that lay over these rugged fields was unbroken, millennia-strong, but nothing more than a deception. Everywhere the struggle continued unabated, unsolved.

Crouch stayed low as the call was answered by a woman's voice.

"Karin? My name is Michael Crouch. Have you heard of me?"

A moment of silence, and then, "I've heard the name, but how do I know you are who you say you are?"

Crouch reeled off a favorite Dinorock quote of Drake's, and Mano Kinimaka's phone number. He also brought her up to speed on the events of the tourney. Karin's silence attested to her shock.

After a moment another voice joined them. "What do you need?"

"I take it you are Komodo? Good. This game they have going is dependent on one thing alone—their ability to control their environment. At the moment they are doing it well—they're prepared. We need to disrupt that advantage."

"How?"

"Take their cyber superiority away from them. Once we have that we own them."

"Sir," Komodo said respectfully. "I get you. But this 'game', as you call it. This is Coyote's challenge. This is her laying down the gauntlet. If we end it too soon won't she just pop up somewhere else, in a month or a year, and make things even harder?"

Crouch agreed, in essence. "Not the point," he said. "We have civilians involved. Local authorities held captive. The threat of brutal force. Even if we feared this woman might slit our throats in our beds a fortnight from now, we should still act to stop this."

"Of course. What's the plan?"

Crouch was about to go over Karin's role but a moment of doubt stopped him. A leader for decades, his competency was currently in question. Who the hell was he to ask this tormented woman to put herself on the line again?

"It's me, isn't it?" She spoke up into the void. "You want me to take down Coyote's network. Damn . . ."

"Do you think you can do it?" Crouch ventured.

"I guess. Do you have any idea how good their circuit boy is?"

Crouch narrowed his eyes. "Their what?"

"Circuit boy. Circuit girl. It's what we hackers used to call ourselves back in the day . . ." she paused. "Maybe still do. Who knows?"

"No ID," Crouch affirmed. "But the guy must be good. If not for what he's already achieved then because Coyote chose him. In itself, that is a bold endorsement."

"Sure," Karin said blandly. "Are they . . . are they in trouble?"

"None more than usual. But they appear to be happy enough. Drake for one finds it easier to fight an axe-wielding madman than fight through the crowds at Meadowhall."

"Yeah, I can't see any of them shopping at the mall."

Crouch took all the emotion out of his voice. "The night will be a long one. Will you do it?"

Karin sighed. "Of course. Of course I'll help them. All of them, even Alicia and Smyth, are my life now. We're family."

Crouch didn't dare speak for a moment. The girl had lost her parents, her brother, but still continued to speak of family so strongly. It made him hate his own weakness.

Eventually, he gave her an address in Leeds and a high-priority password.

"Go now. This will probably be our last communication until this all pans out. Hit 'em hard, Karin, and take no prisoners."

"You have my word."

CHAPTER SIXTEEN

Karin took only a moment to review Crouch's request and then rose quickly to her feet.

"Let's go."

Komodo held up a hand. "We should communicate with Washington. They may be able to help."

"Do it on the way."

Karin forced all thoughts of death and tragedy from her mind. The only way she could help her friends was to give them her full attention, allowing every thought process chance to live and develop and breathe on its own. The demands of cyberwarfare were huge, both on the brain and the subconscious, affecting not only instant cognitive reaction but also those thought processes that matured in the background, usually developing at length into the idea that won you the endgame.

Karin started the car, a rented Mini Cooper, and swerved out into traffic. Horns honked. Karin fiddled with the satnav whilst Komodo called DC. Luckily, the traffic lights through Leeds city center were frequent enough that they didn't need to pull over. Karin took the route past a statue called the Black Prince and accelerated up Kirkstall Road.

Komodo spoke at last. "Smyth? What's going on?"

Her boyfriend listened as Smyth unleased a veritable tirade. Karin cold hear the furious tones clear enough, especially as Komodo had to lift the phone away from his ear.

"Safe house got hit." He shook his head, translating Smyth's bluster. "Everyone's safe. Kinimaka fought an . . . elephant, I think. Smyth did all the work. Saved the day. Fell off a building . . . the usual."

Komodo stopped the man in his tracks with a few choice comments and brought him up to speed. Smyth's rejoinder was surprisingly heated.

"What the hell are the Brits up to? They having Terrorist Amnesty week or something?"

"Coyote has prepared and planned this with the Blood King's help and money," Komodo said. "If the man can kidnap President Coburn he can sure engineer the shutdown of a town for twenty four hours."

"Damn Russkie," Smyth said. "Bastard's in the ground and still haunting us."

Komodo agreed, but didn't say so out loud. Instead he explained Karin's new role as she shot past a Vue cinema and restaurant area, then negotiated a series of bends. Soon, the main road was left behind and darkness closed over the car. Even the streetlights were sparse. Komodo didn't like it, and ended the call saying he would get back to the DC team.

"Where the hell are we?"

Karin shrugged. "Almost there. I trust Crouch. Don't you?"

Komodo grunted. "Drake does. But the man's been compromised for years. How's that affecting him right now?"

"Dunno. Maybe when this is over he and Michael can sit down and talk about it."

Komodo wondered at her brusque tone but ignored it. "Well, it'll take more than a coffee at Starbucks with Crouch to convince me, that's all I'm sayin'."

Karin stopped the car outside a nondescript warehouse. The place was in darkness, streetlights out for blocks around, surrounding businesses either closed down or shut for the night.

A man glided out of the shadows ahead. For all intents and purposes he looked like a local security guard, even to the apparent paunch at his waist. The only things that gave him away was the chiseled face and observant eyes; the hand that never left his pocket. He signaled to Karin to turn the car headlights off.

Komodo climbed out of the car.

"Stop," the guard said, carefully listening to a walkie-talkie and watching the big American.

"Karin Blake?" he asked.

"Not me, dude. She's in the car."

Not impressed, the guard turned away. "Follow me."

CHAPTER SEVENTEEN

Tyler Webb took his seat at the head of the table to chair the second meeting of the Pythians. It came hot on the heels of the first, only days apart; the frequency not a part of his future intentions but necessary to start with.

"We are the Pythians," he said. "Welcome."

His five partners looked suitably smug.

"News," Webb said, sipping from a fluted champagne glass. "What do we have?"

"The grand entrance we spoke of." General Stone spoke up first. "The 'house on the hill' scenario is favored by all and will take a few weeks to prep. Are we pushing ahead?"

Webb was so surprised that they'd all agreed that he caught every eye. Nobody looked away. Stone's scenario was somewhat ruthless, but still, their entry into the game should be a memorable one. "How many casualties?"

Stone shrugged. "No more than three hundred."

"Set it up," Webb said. "But keep the casualty rate down. I don't want an international manhunt to be our first contact with the greater populace. We should show restraint as well as great viciousness when required."

"The only question is—where? Maybe I'll stick a pin in the map."

Webb looked to Robert Norris, executive of SolDyn. "Where are we with Pandora?"

Norris bit delicately into a canapé. "Mmm, exquisite. Please congratulate your chef de cuisine for me."

Webb waited patiently.

Norris got the hint. "Our web spreads well. Manpower is growing. The London plague pit is confirmed but its location still eludes us. More of the puzzle is required, I fear, to narrow it down. At least two other plague pits or sites do exist—in Paris and the US. I still ponder over the US site, though it is apparently confirmed. These other pits are purportedly ancient . . ."

Nicholas Bell, the builder, laughed, spraying a chunk of tasty canapé across the table in front of him. "America didn't just pop up when the Redskins wanted it to," he said, practically choking. "Bubonic plague's been in and out for centuries. Still is."

Several members regarded the builder with distaste. Webb didn't blame them. His antics weren't exactly in keeping with the group. Only General Stone came close to the commoner's low status and even he knew when to adopt the correct protocols. Webb wondered again about resigning the builder to video calls only.

Still, he thought. *The man does offer some amusement.*

"As before," he said. "Work harder. Pandora is everything for now. It will assert our stranglehold on the world. Anything else?"

Clifford Bay-Dale, the officious prick and energy lord, spoke over the top of Miranda Le Brun, the oil heiress. She allowed it with a bored smile.

"How about some of those perks you mentioned, Webb? I believe the shadow rulers of a planet should be receiving bonuses by now."

"We are not the shadow rulers yet," Webb said. "Work first, play later. There is much hard work still to do, Clifford."

Bay-Dale frowned. Maybe it hadn't occurred to him before that his requests could be denied.

Webb swept the table with questioning eyes. "Are we together on this?"

Miranda Le Brun spoke for all of them. "The Pythians are here to stay." She continued in her wearied tones, "There comes a time when those with wealth and power find they have nothing left to learn. No more to discover. No new experiences nor encounters to enjoy. I think, within this group, new horizons may open up. My expectations are high."

Webb smiled. He couldn't have put it better himself, thought did not fully share Le Brun's views. The sum of his life's ambitions were in this group. He was not only committed, he would die to protect it.

"Our day has already begun," he said. "The world just does not know it yet. Put the first strike in position. Oh, and how did Beauregard do in the UK?"

General Stone smiled.

CHAPTER EIGHTEEN

Kinimaka finally breathed a huge sigh of relief. The effort caused him pain; soreness and aches that throbbed from bruise to bruise like phone calls pinging around a network, but he felt the last few hours had answered several worrying questions in the affirmative.

Following the safe house fiasco Robert Price, the new Secretary of Defense, had taken personal charge of the SPEAR team's safety. At first, Kinimaka had felt a jolt of alarm, Smyth had been slightly more vociferous and Hayden's eyes had pinched a little, but they all knew this moment would come sooner or later.

"Better sooner," Hayden had told them. "But don't let your guards down."

Following a clever extraction and a journey in the back of a dark van equipped with medical necessities for Hayden, they arrived at their new destination.

Kinimaka saw it as he opened the van door. His mouth fell open. Smyth voiced his thoughts precisely, "You're shitting me."

Hayden actually sat up. "Now that's more like it."

The Pentagon loomed before them, an imposing concrete structure that, in the flesh, looked nothing like it did on television, which was usually an aerial view. Of course, close up, most visitors only got to see two sides at any one time, some only one.

Inside, they were assigned a room for Hayden and an adjoining office. Kinimaka lost count of their floor number, so concerned was he for his girlfriend. In the end, Hayden had to shoo him away. Kinimaka flinched as he straightened his body.

"Go get some pain killers or something."

"Yeah, and a new penis," Smyth said snappishly. "Your boss has taken charge of your last one."

Hayden snipped at Smyth too. "I'm still in charge, Smyth, so fall into line. I won't listen to that kind of insubordination. Got it?"

Smyth only smiled. "Good to see you're recovering so fast," he said.

Hayden put down the file she'd had her nose in ever since the Secretary of Defense handed it to her, on his way out of the room. "Take a look," he'd said. "Could be your next assignment."

Hayden flapped the file. "Wait, Mano, just a few minutes. This is important. While we're offline, so to speak, other agencies have been monitoring the kind of events that might have fallen within our radar. *This* is the biggest yet. We've heard talk—" she made a face. "More like *chatter* that an organization called The Pythians is starting to make a few waves. Now, we've heard the name before, I know, but never attached to anything more than conjecture. Mystery. It's all been a little cryptic."

"Until now?" Kinimaka asked.

Hayden shrugged. "Nothing concrete. But the NSA reports chatter has increased in *all* the world's hotspots regarding the Pythians. That means something. CIA are poking around too."

"Is that it?" Smyth asked.

"NSA believe they're recruiting. For what, we don't know. Figures that have been approached and then rebuffed the offer, and there are only a handful we could find, make mention of being able to take their pick of three destinations—London, Paris and California."

"For what?"

Hayden sighed. "I guess we'll find out. That's all."

Kinimaka, heading out of the door, stopped in mid-stride as their new internal line began to ring. Very few people had gotten the landline number yet; indeed the circle had been intentionally limited to a select few.

SPEAR members. Robert Price and other high-ranking figures. The people guarding Kono.

"Yes?" Smyth was there first. "What is it?"

The man's face fell as he listened. He held the receiver out to Kinimaka. "It's the FBI in LA. It's about Kono."

Kinimaka's stomach flipped. He snatched at the phone. "What happened?"

"Mano? It's Special Agent Collins. I'm sorry to say that another attempt was made on Kono's life earlier today. She——"

"Is she okay?" Kinimaka all but screamed.

Collins breathed. "She's fine. We took them all out," she paused. "With a little help. But we saved her. You owe me a dance, Mr. Kinimaka."

Kinimaka sat down hard. "Oh, thank God. Thank *you*. And what do you mean—a little help?"

"Ever hear of Aaron Trent?"

Kinimaka surfed his brain waves. "Trent. Trent? Wasn't he part of that CIA group that was disavowed?"

"You got it. Well, Trent, he owes me more than a few dances too and lately he's finally gotten around to settling up. I received the alert from Kono's detail and headed over there, but by the time we arrived on scene half of our team were wounded or dead. Aaron came with me—"

Kinimaka blinked. "Was that wise?"

"Oh, he's good," Collins confessed. "When I first got this LA gig I thought it was all about busting his team's balls, and I came through, believe me. But they're good people. Hard. Clever. Dependable. Damn, I wish half my colleagues were a quarter as good."

"Good to know."

"So, we come upon the scene and the whole house is going up in flames. Masked men can be seen through the windows. I head for the front door. Trent just races and leaps through the shattered window, lands and neutralizes two men before I get to him. The third I pop and we're heading for the stairs. At that point Kono herself comes flying down, on fire. Flames literally blazing up and down her entire back."

Kinimaka closed his eyes, distraught.

"Trent jumps on her, putting her out with his coat and his body. I shoot over the top of their hunched forms, taking down man after man. They collapse down the stairs, already catching fire. We back out. Trent throws Kono over his shoulder. I fend off an overgrown brute with a goatee. We head outside, grabbing what's left of our team. At the start of the driveway we come under fire, bullets hammering the ground around us from the second floor windows. We're trapped for as long as those goons realize the house is burning down all around them, until they get the message that they're actually gonna die screaming." She paused and took another breath.

"Still," she breathed. "Doesn't help us. We'd be dead in about two more minutes. The goons have autos trained on us. The only reason they haven't hit us is because they're fucking useless shots and we're crouched down low like a row of husbands during a brothel raid. All is lost. And then . . ."

Kinimaka's eyes were wide. "Yes?"

"The rest of the Disavowed show up like fuckin' super heroes. Silk and his new woman, a cop called Brewster, and Dan Radford. They peppered that house with 16mms, round after round, obliterating the goons from the face of the earth. Man, I've lost count of the number of battles I've fought with those guys, but they always take it to the max."

"Thank you," Kinimaka whispered. "Thank them for me. Is Kono with you now?"

"No, she's at Radford's place. Don't worry, he's back with his wife. Again."

Kinimaka didn't know what to say. His most heartfelt thanks wouldn't do this justice. Instead he gave her what he could. "Whatever you guys need. Anywhere. Anytime. Just ask. The SPEAR team is well connected in DC . . . for now," he added as an afterthought. "Don't hesitate to call me."

Collins laughed. "I won't."

Kinimaka replaced the receiver in its cradle and looked around. "Kono was attacked again but she's okay. By the Great Kahuna's balls I'll be glad when this is all over."

Hayden checked the time. "Won't be long," she said. "I wonder how they're doing."

CHAPTER NINETEEN

Drake checked his wrist. "Damn, I'll never get used to not wearing a watch."

"I don't believe I've ever seen you with a timepiece on your wrist," Dahl said.

"Not since I left the regiment," Drake said. "Long time now, mate."

"Are you hinting?" Mai asked lightly. "I don't take hints very well."

"Hear, hear," Alicia mumbled.

The rumbles and bursts of arms had died away. The team had considered rushing to the aid of the locals, but had decided the four remaining assassins and the upcoming arrival of Coyote was the greater priority. Dahl was engrossed in his big piece of plastic.

"I have two signals now at the castle," he said. "Neither moving. On the one hand these two could have become trapped by each other, neither wanting to make the first move, which is kind of ironic. On the other they could both be dug in waiting for somebody to test them."

Alicia made a pretense of shielding her eyes and looking up at the castle. "Let's not disappoint them."

Drake agreed. "It's oh two hundred hours. Most of the town is asleep. The castle is a safe place to fight."

"Let's hope none of the local youths think so too." Alicia followed Dahl up a narrow alleyway.

"If they do," Drake's disembodied voice said behind her. "It'll either kill 'em or cure 'em."

Up they went until the alleyway opened onto a wider road, bordered by houses and garages. It was the kind of street where the front windows of a house practically sat above the sidewalk, not good for the privacy of residents or would-be skulkers. The four of them passed swiftly, soon reaching the top of the hill and approaching the castle walls.

The battlements were high where they still stood intact, cracked and crumbled in other places. A shallow moat encircled the walls. Drake spied a gate to the left. Dahl pointed to the right.

"Walls are so damaged over there we could sneak across."

Drake nodded. "All ways in are compromised," he said. "We make the best of it."

It was all they could do. None of them wanted to be here, forcibly pitted against hardened killers, but it wasn't in any of them to lurk and hide. Leave that for prowlers, cutthroats and gutter rats. Drake led the way across a deteriorated, jagged wall, squeezing between the broken stones and slipping down the other side onto a well-cut sward of grass. Instantly, he crouched down in the shadows cast by the wall, surveying the area. The castle was almost circular, its walls irregular. A tall keep sat in the middle, broken-down but with its remains standing on top of a high hillock. A manmade wooden switchback staircase led to the top. Beyond it was a delve in the earth, almost like a wide drain, that led to an original barred grating and several seemingly irregular portions of inner wall, most of them covered in rustling foliage.

Drake cast around, feeling exposed. Dahl crouched next to him, tracking device in hand. "If they've seen us," the Swede said. "Surely they will move." He checked his watch. "Twelve minutes is up."

He switched the screen on, taking in the flashing dots. "Still two in the castle. Almost on top of each other, but the scale is relatively small. One of them—" he glared hard at the screen. "Is in the very center of the castle." He looked up at the high keep. "There."

Drake searched through the gloom at the top of the grassy hill. To make matters worse the battered remains of the structure up there offered many low walls to hide behind and two tall, jagged rocky rectangles.

"Any clues?"

"Hey, Mai's the bloody ninja," Alicia hissed. "Send her up. I'd be amazed if she doesn't come down with the assassin's head *and* another small child. Ah, screw it."

With that Alicia started up the steep slope. Instantly, the challenge was accepted. From the murk above a heavy, sudden boom rang out, a deep, resonating twang like an industrial strength rubber band being fired and Drake saw something lift into the night.

"What the hell—"

"Move!" Dahl shouted, recognition in his voice. "It's a Net Gun."

Drake scrambled. He did not want to be there when the thing landed. Like a spider's web it arced through the night, tiny weights attached to its edges, dozens of individual threads glistening with a barely lighter shade of dark as they flew toward them. The net seemed to soar for ten minutes, hanging in space, but only seconds passed before it thunked down hard. Drake and the others were clear, an outside strand slipping over Alicia's foot but not catching.

"He's had time to set up a good defense," Dahl said.

And then the assassin at the top of the hill proved it. Manic laughter rang out and small glow sticks were thrown haphazardly down the hill. Following them came actual bouncing bombs; grenades already primed and thrown at irregular intervals so they exploded at different times.

The team scrambled for cover. One grenade exploded near the top of the hill, sending up a shower of sod and dirt. Another rolled for several more seconds, its boom resonating through the ground. Yet another passed by the team, detonating behind them. Drake hugged the ground as it discharged its deadly firepower, then looked up.

"Crap. There's more!"

And still they came. Chance wouldn't stay forever on their side. Drake pointed to the sturdy wooden bridge that led to the staircase up the hill and ran for it, seeing Mai at his side. Dahl had already broken the other way, circumventing the mound, heading for the assassin's blind side, and Alicia had taken off after him.

Drake reached the relative safety and impenetrable darkness underneath the bridge and stairway. Another explosion shook the castle's foundations. Solid timber planks shook and dislodged flurries of debris, raining it over their hair and shoulders. Drake didn't stay put for long. They had to keep moving forward.

Mai grabbed his shoulder and pointed. The stairway led to the very top of the hill and provided great cover. Drake nodded. Their quarry would not guess how fast they could be. He set off, head down, scanning the ground as much as the dismal light would allow. Stones and clods of earth dislodged in his wake. Mai stepped lightly at his back. Behind and to their sides even more grenades were detonated. Twice, fragments of earth spattered under the bridge, stinging their exposed flesh. The structure shook, but held firm. Drake reminded himself that Dahl and Alicia were most likely assaulting the keep from another angle. The assassin would know he was under attack.

He's had plenty of time to plan this.

What else could they do? Time was their enemy. Coyote was coming. The townspeople might even soon be dragged into this, and then all bets and potential outcomes were thrown into a highly volatile mix. Add some kind of terrorist response unit to that . . .

Drake ran harder, almost fell, but caught himself on a solid wooden support. A grenade bounced so close they heard it skipping along the turf to their right. It detonated seconds later.

The stairway juddered. Drake and Mai were thrown to the ground. Drake rose immediately, soil and bits of grass streaming from his shoulders. "Damn, that was—"

Mai hissed a warning before he heard it. Grenades tossed *under the bridge*, rolling toward them.

Before they could react, the bombs exploded. Drake pushed his body down as far as the soft, yielding earth would allow. But that was only a precaution; he knew the rolling, bumpy terrain above them would help shield the blast.

The real problem was the stairway collapsing all around them.

Timbers, spars and support columns groaned and twisted, planks crashed to the earth or flew into the air depending how close they were to the blast radius. Reinforcement joists cracked. A spear of timber drove hard into the ground three feet to Drake's left. He dashed that way, crablike, knowing through instinct that Mai would break right. A thick length of six-by-two slammed down onto his trailing leg, landing face-side first so that the impact was lessened. Nevertheless, Drake felt the blow in every nerve, issuing a deep grunt. When an ominous crack sounded above he rolled blindly, in a sudden snapshot seeing his hand caught underneath collapsing planks, amazed when they smashed down to either side of his wrist, leaving him untouched.

He rolled on, into the open. The stairway collapsed behind him, toppling and crashing down even as more grenades exploded within it, sending new splinter- and plank-filled plumes high into the air, and far and wide. Drake rolled to his knees immediately to get his bearings, a little shocked to see he was three-quarters of the way up the hill, only twenty strides from the top.

Above and to the right he could see Mai, already pounding the grass, fleet of foot as if nothing had happened.

He pushed up, tired of this game of king of the hill. In that moment the figure of a man appeared at the top.

"Duster's me name! Blimey, come and get me!" he cried. "Killin's me game! Chow down on this, ya Yorkshire twat! 'Nuff said."

Drake barely heard the insult, not that he could have translated it particularly well. He'd already seen the three-cylinder backpack strapped to Duster's back, the long lance of the gun aiming toward him, and the horrific potential of what was about to happen.

"Flamethrower!" he cried at the top of his lungs.

This would be no old, out-of-date model, this would be a contemporary killing machine. In the movies, flamethrowers were depicted as having a short range, mostly to preserve the actors' safety. In real life they could extend a spout of flame almost eight meters. Drake threw himself back down the hill, hearing a whoosh of flame at his back. The plus points of a man using a flamethrower meant that his mobility was impaired and the weapon's burn time was severely limited. All this gave Mai and Dahl and Alicia more of a chance.

But Duster would be aware of that.

Trying to second-guess a killer of this caliber was like galloping through a littered minefield, but again the team had no choice. Drake felt the hot air at his back, swiveled and watched as the flame expended itself. Then he was up again, covering the scorched earth and stamping in between the mini-fires that lit up the dark for yards around. Mai had already reached the summit. Drake saw Duster's figure and heard his rant.

"Wotcher, me old friend! What 'ave yew got fer me? Sorted!"

Duster had unstrapped the cylinders, letting the bulk fall heavily to the floor, and now threw the lance toward Mai. Then, like a cowboy, he whipped out two guns from twin holsters at his sides, firing each one quickly, dramatically and with an unmistakable flourish.

Mai threw herself sideways, bullets passing inches above her body. Drake knew even she couldn't survive another salvo from Duster's trusty weapons. He hurled the only weapon he had—his knife—toward the assassin. Forced to act quickly, its arc wasn't good; it clashed against Duster's arm handle first, but at least gave the man a moment's pause.

A shot rang out. That would be Dahl firing his handgun. The noose was closing.

Duster grinned. Drake cringed when he saw it.

What . . . ?

Duster threw some kind of miniature flickering flame. Instantly a circle of fire ignited all around him, shooting up over six feet high. Drake figured the circle was about ten feet across, giving the man ample room to move. But flames wouldn't stop bullets.

Dahl fired again, but Drake was able to distinguish nothing through the flames as he reached the top of the hill. The asshole had probably gone to ground. With that thought barely completed, the night erupted again, this time in the form of more bouncing bombs.

Not aimed at Drake's team . . .

They exploded at the bases of the various crumbling walls that ringed the top of the hill. Though ruined, they were in parts still quite tall and now came crashing down. Three high walls collapsed, rolling gently before tumbling faster and faster. Dahl was under one, Mai another. The Swede saw the danger and pounded away, head down, but even so it was his instincts that kept him alive. As the plummeting wall descended toward him he threw a forearm up, deflecting the heavy block that would have split his skull. The rest of the blocks smashed down inches behind his fleeing ankles, shaking the earth with their destruction.

Duster cackled through it all.

Mai picked up top speed almost immediately, anticipating the trajectory of the crumpling edifice. The blocks never came near her, but at the end of her sprint she tucked herself into a ball and simply launched herself into the flames.

Drake gawped. "No!"

He ran closer, as near as he dared go, squinting and sweating as a wall of heat pushed him back. The height of the flames had decreased; they were dying down. Just at the edge of his line of sight he saw Torsten Dahl following Mai's lead, barreling toward the searing curtain and leaping through.

Drake stepped back. "Bollocks to it."

With a short run up he too dared the blaze. Sharp, sizzling tongues licked at him from every angle, hungry for flesh. A brief crackling sound struck his ears, striking a fervent desire inside that the sound wasn't his own burning flesh.

He landed on two feet, still running, hot but alive, charred maybe, but still on mission. Duster was in the process of rising from his prone position. Mai angled toward him. Dahl came from another angle.

"What the hell were you thinking?" Drake managed, panting.

"Got tired of waiting," she said.

"Wotcher," Duster cried, madness in his voice as he stood up to the odds. "Bin waiting to try this little baby out f'meself fer weeks. Now it's bagged me five million quid."

Drake saw in his hand a black plastic box and beneath his thumb a tiny red button.

Mai sprang for his throat.

"No!"

CHAPTER TWENTY

Mai ploughed into Duster at chest height. The look of surprise flew across the assassin's face almost as fast as the plastic box flew out of his hands. Drake fought the choices—help Mai or try to secure the box. If it landed red-button down the odds weren't good for survival.

Dahl had veered toward the box, an eager fielder racing for the catch of the game.

Drake ran and slid in. Duster hit the ground as Drake arrived, eating a good chunk of boot and dirt for his trouble. Mia's leap had taken her beyond the two of them, and now she landed cat-like, already turning.

Duster groaned.

Drake let his eyes flick toward Dahl. Even Duster was trying to see what happened, cringing slightly.

Dahl flung himself forward, one hand out, as the plastic box came down to earth. Tumbling, tumbling, it hit, but Dahl's palm was there to catch it before it landed. Furthermore, he managed to grip its square edges, preventing the little red button from striking his palm.

"Fucker landed face down," Drake shook his head. "Always does."

Dahl's outstretched hand gripped the trigger harder now, the button a hair's breadth from his skin. He sat up, grinning. "You're out." He nodded at Duster.

Alicia's voice could be heard through the dwindling flames. "Are you idiots all right in there? What the hell's going on?"

But Duster wasn't done yet. With stamina born of years of hardship and fighting he rolled and jumped to his feet, running hard for the wall of flame. Drake knew the assassin could have traps and stashes all over the castle; allowing him his freedom wasn't an option. Thinking on his feet, he grabbed one of the big, tumbled wall stones and flung it at the man's back. The blow sent him reeling, straight through the flames and staggering across the other side.

"At last," they heard Alicia say. "Something to hit."

Alicia made short work of the assassin, holding him up by the hair as Drake, Mai and finally Dahl made their way over. The wall of flames had all but dwindled to nothing, allowing shrouds of darkness to creep back across the land.

"Shall we tie him up?" Alicia said dubiously. "Or just throw him off one of the battlements?"

"Tie him up?" Drake echoed. "You've brought rope?"

"Handcuffs." Alicia smiled wickedly. "Never know when they might be useful."

"Let's try that," Dahl said. "And—"

The snapping report of a gunshot cracked the night apart, echoing around the castle walls. Duster collapsed in a spray of blood, half his head blown away. Drake dived for the floor.

"We're sitting ducks up here!"

"There were two signals." Dahl hit the dirt beside him, still holding the detonator. "Why wait this long?"

"It is the coward's way," Mai said. "This assassin will have been hoping Duster would do the hard work first, then step in after."

"That way," Alicia said, nodding at the eastern slope. "Shot came from the west."

Drake slithered off. As he passed Duster a hand slammed down on his own, grasping hard. "V . . . Vin . . . it is the . . ."

Drake gripped the man's hand hard. Foe or not, a man about to die passed easier with a little compassion.

"All right, mate. It's all right."

Duster's vision cleared for a brief second. "Vincent," he said. "The Ghost."

Drake nodded. Blood pooled in the grass around the man's head. His passing was marked by nothing more than the sudden slump of his shoulders; the expected lot of a paid killer. The other three were already over the summit of the hill by the time Drake looked up and started to follow.

"What did he say?" Alicia asked.

"The shooter is Vincent, The Ghost. The notes said he likes to make use of his terrain to stay hidden; that he can wait unmoving for days until the perfect opportunity arises."

Dahl made a speculative face. "Around that side of the castle are a few crumbling walls, a partly broken-down structure, the culvert, and the stumps of other walls long since gone to wrack and ruin. Also the ticket office."

"One wrong move and that bastard will pick us off," Alicia said.

"Stay close."

Mai moved off, hugging the grassy hill as if it were her last hope. She angled downward as she crept along, slinking even further into shadow. Their adversary couldn't know which direction they'd take, and Mai went the long way around. As Drake followed he saw her plan. Whilst still not a great advantage, she led them toward the deep culvert that led to the rusted old gate. The depth of the culvert would help shield them and get them closer to Vincent's lair.

Wherever that was.

The team climbed down the slope and entered the culvert, slipping down to the bottom. The grass was a little wet down here, the ground soft. The sides were slick and could become a hindrance. The group kept low, moving out of the shadow of the hill and able to carefully view the western side of the castle's grounds. Sure enough, Drake saw a discontinuous ruin of inner castle walls, one covered by foliage; enough dips and hillocks to hide a circus; a ramshackle structure; and the modern timber-built ticket office. Not to mention the battlements and even more leafy foliage and shadow coating the far castle wall.

The team watched, observed. All they needed was a glimmer.

"Getting on for oh three thirty hours," Alicia said into the silence. "We have to end this soon if we're still set on ruining the Coyote bitch's grand entrance."

"If Vincent's dug in," Dahl whispered. "He could stay hidden until I'm doing my victory lap."

Drake scratched his head. "Who? You?"

"Well, we can't just crawl on outta here and leave him behind," Alicia hissed.

Drake eyed her, sudden hope lighting his face. "Now there's a plan."

They convinced Alicia that since it was her plan, she should be the one to carry it out. The Englishwoman only rolled her eyes and sighed, but left the departing comment that they should stop trying to be smart and pull it together. Truth be told, Drake did feel that the long, tense night was starting to take its toll. He gave Alicia one of their two guns and made sure he reminded her to pick up Duster's on her way out of the castle.

They waited.

It didn't take long. Drake, Mai and Dahl carefully found comfortable vantage points and set about surveying the entire western side between them. The night's silence was unbroken, lending an air of isolation to proceedings that frayed their nerves even further. Absolute stillness was essential; Drake was just glad it wasn't your typical brisk and rainy English night.

A gun was fired, the shot echoing far and wide, but clearly some distance away. Then a shout and another shot—this one coming from a different gun. The caliber of the bullet told the tale to any experienced ear. Six seconds later and another bullet was fired.

Drake waited. Their ruse had been played. It made sense that if Vincent fell for the deception he would break cover. Either way, he'd take only minutes to decide.

Not a blade of grass stirred. A hush like the calm before the storm enveloped the castle. Twenty seconds passed, then thirty. Drake could imagine Alicia becoming impatient, wondering if she should let loose another salvo. He prayed she didn't. Vincent would surely recognize overkill.

"It didn't work," Dahl said.

Drake cursed inwardly. *What next?*

Then, eagle-eyed Mai focused on a particular spot. Drake could see by the set of her shoulders, the sudden tensing, that she'd spotted something. He squinted as best he could in the same direction, but saw only black layered upon deeper black. All of it covered in hanging foliage.

Bit by bit, Mai turned to Dahl. "Run," she whispered.

The Swede's jaw hit the ground. "What? Are you insane? He'd pick me off in three seconds."

"I only need two," she said grimly. "Now. Run."

"Well, sorry, but that's still cutting it a little bit fine. How about Drake? He's fast and dumb."

"That might have worked," Drake admitted, "if I wasn't standing next to you."

Mai fixed the man with questioning eyes. "Are you losing it, Dahl?"

The Swede's jaw picked itself up and set hard. "If you're sure?"

"Trust me."

Dahl did. Drake could see it in the man's eyes. He doubted there was another person on earth Dahl would put so much faith in. If Mai said she could pull the trigger one second before Vincent, then that was good enough.

"Ready?"

Dahl took a deep breath and set himself. Mai readied their last weapon and clenched a fist. When she relaxed it, Dahl exploded into action. Dirt flew from the heels of his boots as he sprinted from full dark to partial dark. Vincent The Ghost was a sharpshooter and would be on him already, tracking for the perfect shot. Dahl's life would be measured in the next few seconds.

Mai never wavered. Her concentration was absolute. Drake counted the seconds, every nerve in his body strained to the limit.

One . . . two . . .

Nothing happened.

Shit . . . Dahl!

. . . thr . . .

A shot rang out. Drake's ears rang, signaling that it was from Mai's gun. Despite having his eyes glued to the same spot as Mai he never saw a thing, but the Japanese woman caught a flicker, a darkness that shouldn't be there, an odd shape that seemed somewhat alien.

It moved, just a trace, a fine adjustment of a sensitive sight perhaps, giving Mai the target. She fired. Dahl dropped to the ground.

Something fell from the foliage clinging to the ruined castle walls. At first appearance it was a leafy monster, an indeterminate shape dropping like a shapeless sack. Mai broke cover, her weapon still aimed. Dahl looked up from where he'd dropped.

Drake grinned. "Did ya break anything in your heroic dive?"

Dahl ignored him, staring at the bizarre clump. "Is that him?"

Mai moved in closer, gun arm steady, very much aware that this man was an elusive wraith—an international assassin prone to acts of misdirection. In a moment of doubt she pumped two more bullets into the mass, just in case.

Drake nodded. "Good move."

They approached slowly. Drake whistled his admiration as Vincent's elaborate disguise became clearer. The man had coated himself, top to bottom, in foliage then fashioned a little perch among the leaves and other greeneries that grew up the castle wall. He even wore a leafy helmet and the barrel of his gun was covered and dulled with vegetation.

"The Ghost," Mai said. "I see why."

"How the hell did you see him?" Drake asked.

"You can disguise and cover up all you want," Mai said. "But you can't hide your eyes. Not if you want to see your target."

"You saw a glint in his eye from all the way over there?" Drake shook his head.

"You didn't?"

"Must have been the angle," Drake muttered. "Still, that's another one down."

Alicia came running up to them. "C'mon!" she cried. "Didn't you hear the screams?"

Drake let his focus spread out. Terrified screams drifted on the air, setting the night on edge. The citizens of Sunnyvale were in trouble.

Alicia ran ahead. "It's coming from the supermarket."

CHAPTER TWENTY ONE

The clock ticked, moving closer to that 0600 hours pivotal point when Coyote would enter the fray. The enormous impact and potential consequences of that single act faded into the background for now as Drake heard the terrified screams coming up from the town below. The team hurried along the benighted streets, even now forced to leave nothing to chance. Assassins continued to stalk the shadows and the team had to be vigilant every step of the way. Drake knew the position of the supermarket, understanding immediately why Alicia had pinpointed it. Nothing else of any note stood out that way, save for a large parking area. What worried him was that at this time, the supermarket should have long since been deserted.

They lingered around hedgerows that clung like motorcycle sidecars to the bend that opened up on its way to the supermarket. The cries had died down by now, but Drake could still hear the low pleas of the trapped and deep groans of those in pain.

Almost on cue a voice rang out, distorted and boosted by the building's public address system. "Drake and team. I give you five minutes then we try again. Five minutes to show yourselves and surrender to me." A pause, then, "If not . . ." A scream rang out.

Drake tensed. Mai's hand fell on his shoulder. "Wait. We have five minutes."

"But—"

"We have five minutes."

Drake's natural instinct was always to rush to the aid of the innocent, those dragged into hardship and warfare through no fault of their own. But Mai was right. To rush in now was to lose whatever slight advantage they may have. Waiting gave them options.

"We need a plan," Dahl said unnecessarily.

"Well, I got plan B covered," Alicia smiled mirthlessly. "Storm the place."

"The accent," Mai said. "I think Israeli. This would be Blackbird then, the Mossad operative."

"Didn't think Mossad would stoop this low," Drake grumped.

"Who knows?" Mai said. "Could be rogue. Either way, they would never admit anything. And their operatives are notoriously hard to break. The only people we actualy know that want you dead over in that general part of the world are all those terrorists you ambushed at the arms bazaar in the Czech Republic."

Drake clicked his teeth. "That was some time ago now, but the death threats are constant and very real. I thought they might forget about me. *Us*! I guess all those terrorists will want some kind of reckoning."

Mai's face took on a fatalistic expression. "Enemies may get older, but they never forget."

"Can we focus on now?" Dahl said. "This Blackbird person is going to start dishing out pain again very soon."

Alicia pointed to nearby houses where doors stood open and windows were smashed. "Looks like he dragged people out from their houses."

"Which limits the hostage count," Drake said. "We still need a visual."

"So what do we do?" Dahl wondered.

"What we always do," Drake answered. "We go save the day."

The condition of the supermarket gave them more answers. The front door was shattered, hanging off its hinges. The windows around it were also smashed. No alarm wailed, so they had to guess Blackbird had managed to improvise a bypass. Through the wrecked frontage the team observed three people pressed up against the glass windows at the far side of the supermarket, hands and faces touching the panes.

"Front's clear," Drake said. "And even more clearly a trap."

"No time to wait. No chance to negotiate," Mai said. "What to do?"

"Take out the hostages," Alicia said quietly.

"*What?*"

"They're his only leverage. So let's take 'em out."

"*How?* And when you say 'take out' . . ."

Alicia spun her two handguns and proceeded to break cover and walk out into the open. "Like this. Bye bye hostages."

And she opened fire, aiming at the very window where the hostages stood. The whole pane fractured and smashed before collapsing like a waterfall. Pieces littered the pathway, a sudden sharp tide. The hostages shrieked and fell back inside, away from the danger, quickly diving to the floor.

Alicia was among them in seconds, Drake and Mai backing her up. Mai pulled the hapless trio outside and handed them off to Dahl.

Drake and Alicia took point, crouching in the sudden stillness and sensing the very air of the place. Racks of shelves stretched away toward the rear of the place, full of produce and materials. The faint night-time illumination lent a stark aura to the large space, making it feel even more unfriendly.

A trolley rolled slowly down one of the aisles. Drake noticed the package nestled inside a moment before Alicia.

"Down!"

They hit the deck. The package exploded a few seconds later—not a massive explosion but a charge filled with enough firepower to have taken them out had it struck true. Drake rolled as one of the supermarket shelves toppled, sending hundreds of items tipping and toppling to the floor. A stand of paperbacks and DVDs tumbled too, hitting the main row of cash registers. Several of the tills must have been left on, as Drake heard the ding of barcodes being registered.

He shifted. Blackbird, clad in pure black, was already racing *along the top of the next row of shelving*, bent almost double. Startled by the sight, and by the shape, he took a moment to process the attack.

By then Blackbird was airborne, moving too fast for him to react in time. The masked figure was on him and all he could do was raise an arm to ward off the inevitable attack. Collapsing under the weight of his opponent, he managed to squirm out from underneath. Blackbird was fast, swiveling and striking all in one single movement. Drake again caught the blow.

Last Man Standing

Alicia struck at Blackbird from behind.

The masked assassin turned. Drake heard the words, "Crazy Englishwoman," emerge from their opponent's mouth and thought, *Welcome to Alicia's world.* Blackbird struck time and time again but Alicia countered every blow. Drake saw steel flash in the Israeli's hand—he was plucking a blade from a pocket hidden at the base of his spine—and he cried out a warning.

Alicia flipped away. Mai stepped in.

The ex-ninja held her gun steady. The Israeli's disembodied voice sounded surprised. "I thought you the most honorable opponent, Mai Kitano."

"Not tonight," Mai said. "There is too much at risk."

Drake tried a new tack. "Surrender to us now. And we'll let you live."

"I think not. A British prison would not suit me, and your treatment can be as rough as any I have encountered."

Drake held up his hands. "Bollocks to this. What the hell are you gonna do?"

A self-satisfied grunt came through the mask. "I thought you'd be better prepared, SPEAR Team. Didn't you know? *Blackbird never fights alone.*"

Even as the words were spoken, black ropes slithered from the unlit heights of the supermarket ceiling, slapping against the floor seconds before masked figures abseiled down. Drake and Mai and Alicia suddenly found themselves beset by five more able opponents.

All hell broke loose.

A melee of unbelievable proportions erupted across every aisle of the building. Drake leapt at Blackbird. Mai engaged three of the newcomers, and Alicia sprinted at the remaining two with an exultant snarl on her face. Here was battle and bloodshed, hand to hand, fist to fist, the outlet for all her agonies.

Drake pushed Blackbird back down the first aisle. Mai hit her adversaries so hard and with so much guile that all four of them careened into the high shelving itself, toppling it backwards so that the entire length crashed heavily to the floor. Piles of cans and bottles and cereal boxes spilled and surged in all directions. Assassins landed amidst exploding heaps of cereal and busted open carbonated drinks, sprayed with a mixture of soda, orange and fruits of the forest.

Mai picked her way toward them.

Alicia threw a heavy can at her first opponent, a little stunned when the figure just nutted it aside.

"Wow. I'm impressed."

She then hefted an unboxed on-sale slow cooker and hurled that in the same direction. "See how you get on with that, motherfucker."

Drake tussled with Blackbird across the floor. The pair rolled across a heap of broken glass; luckily the Israeli was beneath him and was the one grunting in pain. Drake pressed his advantage, freeing his hands with a sudden jerk and then striking at his opponent's weak points. He was momentarily surprised to find those areas reinforced by the special suit.

He shouldn't have been. This was Mossad after all.

Blackbird came back with several deadly blows. Drake repelled them all but found himself driven back against one of the tills. Quickly, he jumped and skimmed across the conveyor belt bouncing his feet off the cash register and rolling aside. By the time Blackbird caught him he was up again, more prepared than previously.

Alicia's first adversary had succumbed to the slow-cooker attack. Her second came at her fast, but appeared to be put off by having to pick his way through an uneven jumble of groceries. Alicia didn't let it faze her one bit. She had fought harder opponents in worse places then this. She trampled through the mishmash, trusting her inner balance and training to make the necessary adjustments. Using the clutter to her advantage, she kicked cereal boxes at her opponent's masked face, then dove in low, took the guy's legs away and smashed his nose against the floor. With a limitless supply of weapons at hand, Alicia upended a two liter bottle of Pepsi over the mask whilst holding the head in place.

"Cola-boarded," she said speculatively. "Wonder if it's a world first?"

Mai was falling back toward Drake, beset by the three assassins. Two of them moved stiffly, clearly carrying injuries, but they were competent enough to carry the fight to Mai.

Another row of shelving toppled, smashing to the floor and emptying its contents in a wide, messy spread. One of Mai's assailants was caught underneath, groaning as their leg was trapped. An errant metal strut glanced off Mai's head, drawing a bead of blood and momentarily distracting her. Instantly, the other two leapt. Mai battled them off, but fell to her knees.

Drake pushed Blackbird as hard as he could, aware of his companions' own struggles, but the Israeli was no slouch, matching him blow for blow and strategy for strategy.

They needed an edge.

As if hearing the silent call, a large figure suddenly filled the broken supermarket doorway.

"So what's all this?" Torsten Dahl said. "Looks like I'm missing out on all the fun."

The Swede pelted forward like a runaway juggernaut, taking one of Mai's remaining opponents by surprise. The guy just stood there and let the Swede ram him, as if disbelieving he would actually go through with it. Dahl laughed as he collided with the assassin.

"You don't play chicken with the Mad Swede," he said. "What the hell happened here? Blackbird clone himself or something?"

Drake let loose a flurry of blows. "Something like that."

"Hey." Alicia moved up behind the Israeli. "You're out of boyfriends."

Dahl motioned to Mai that she should join them, and she faced her last opponent with a grin. When the man charged him, Dahl wrenched a piece of shelving away from its metal housing and smacked him on the side of the head with it; a batter striking a home run.

The last of Blackbird's assistant assassins dropped like a stone.

Drake gave the man a moment. "You're a tough bastard, I'll give you that. But you're alone now. Time to give it up."

Around them, the devastated store creaked and groaned. Precarious piles shifted. Blackbird held out his hands.

"I give up."

"Why are you here? What's Mossad doing mixed up in all this?" Mai asked.

Blackbird shrugged. "I personally just wanted to try my hand against the best team in the world. Mossad? It looks at the bigger picture. The global account. Stupendous and very dark things are starting to happen in the wider world, my friends. Power-hungry men that would rule us—all are taking sides and making plays. It has already begun."

"What things?" Drake asked.

"This group, the Pythians, and others, believe much is connected. Pandora. The Lionheart. Pyramids. Triangles. It all leads to the greatest, most mind-blowing discovery of our time. Actually, of any time. Even more staggering than your gods."

Drake remembered the Pythian name. He'd considered them a continuation of the Shadow Elite, nothing more. "These guys have some kind of master plan?"

"They do." Blackbird nodded. "But I have said too much already. Now is not the time. Will you free us?"

Drake had been aware that Blackbird's cohorts were rising, and that they all stood immobile, non-threatening. The other Israelis hadn't even brought a knife to the party.

"You endangered innocents. Terrorized them."

Blackbird chuckled. "Thieves," he said. "Do you think we would be so amateur as to smash that door? Did the Swede let them go?"

Drake glanced at Dahl, who spread his hands. "It seems so."

"Well, they won't come back in a hurry."

Drake made the decision. "And neither will you. Leave now. Leave the town, leave the country. But stay in touch. We might be able to help each other."

"We will speak again." With that Blackbird and his team vacated the supermarket. Drake looked around.

"Didn't see that coming."

A new figure entered through the broken doors. Drake almost launched an attack before seeing it was Michael Crouch, back from the field.

"Why on earth are you all standing around?" he asked. "Don't you know? It's oh six hundred hours. Coyote has joined the fight."

CHAPTER TWENTY TWO

Coyote made ready, and entered the dark streets. The field had been narrowed, the cream had risen to the top. Only SPEAR, Beauregard, Crouch and possibly Blackbird remained, though Coyote suspected several unscripted antics had been played out amongst some of the contestants throughout the night.

It mattered not. The endgame was coming. And Coyote was on the hunt.

She checked her equipment, particularly the tracking device. An accumulation of dots were flashing over by the supermarket, but they were already on the move. Her own device was a little more sophisticated than the others—enabling her to upload data onto the system. Such was her intent now as she stopped among the town's many gravestones under a coal-black sky.

"As promised," she whispered to the night.

The tournament's most lucrative take-down (her own choice of course), masked the screen and tapped in a few commands. At first she'd been reluctant to trial Tyler Webb's nano-vests, but when Kovalenko had failed the first test run in the tunnels beneath DC, Coyote had risen to the new challenge. Granted, they were strapped this time to the bodies of four unfortunate civilians instead of President Coburn, but that hardly mattered to her. Webb was influential, powerful, and intent on ruling the world. Coyote would gain the most formidable asset of her career if she tested them for him.

Of course, why me? Why here and now? She harbored the smidgen of an idea that *she* was being tested, as Webb tested all his allies, rather than the vests.

She tapped out a quick message on her burner phone, then sent it via text to the remaining contestants.

Coyote engaged. Nano-vests live. Look for the four green dots. Two hours to detonation—what fun!

That should get Drake tripping. The Yorkshireman was a big fan of the innocent, he hated getting anyone dragged in that shouldn't be there. And he had every right to feel that way, of course. Many people that loved military men and women were innocent, and many of them died.

Coyote flashed back once again to the night his wife died. Coyote tended and nurtured an inner garden—or pit of despair—where all her worst regrets were buried. Alyson Drake was one of the biggest. And it wasn't simply her death, or the accident of it; there was much more to the entire incident than that.

It was the only time as Coyote that Shelly Cohen had thought about giving up her evil persona. The closest she ever came. A last flirtation with redemption. The decision hung in the balance, a guillotine hanging by a frayed thread, and when the blade dropped it mapped out the rest of her life.

Good or evil?

Fate had taken all choice away from her. Shelly Cohen became Coyote forever on that horribly significant night. The façade had consumed her, eating away morals like a maggot devouring flesh. Now, the flashing green dots before her represented just that—dots. A means to an end. They were about as human to her mind as the piece of plastic they transmitted from.

Real people? She killed real people for breakfast.

With the text message sent, Coyote regarded her own tracking device. Another improvement was that hers updated in real-time, not every twelve minutes as the SPEAR team and Beauregard's did. She watched now as four red dots moved quickly toward one of the green ones. How predictable. How admirable.

How insane.

The name of her tournament was Last Man Standing. It was time to claim the title.

CHAPTER TWENTY THREE

Torsten Dahl read Coyote's text message with a shake of his head. The sheer madness of some people blew his mind. True, he had earned the nickname 'The Mad Swede' after performing more than one death-defying feat of bravery in the heat of battle, but this was a whole different league. This was psychopathic and murderous, not even warfare. If this Coyote had ever possessed a heart, it had long since crumbled to ash.

Dahl was a spontaneous man. Given to sudden heroic deeds and hair-raising stunts in battle, he was also prone to crazy, impulsive acts on his family days. Anything from jumping into swimming pools, fully clothed, and getting Johanna, the kids and himself thrown out of their hotel, to impromptu fifty-mile mad dashes for specialist ice cream. It was his crazy, unplanned side that Johanna had originally fallen in love with, though not when she heard he applied the same methods in the Army too.

He tended to keep that part quiet.

They were a happy, fit family. Dahl had met his wife at the gym. His regimen impressed her; his muscles too. When she heard him speak she backed away, wary, no doubt thinking him some kind of shiny-arse local with a rich daddy and a handful of procured well-paid jobs to peruse.

Actually, Dahl kept it quiet from everyone except her that he'd dropped out of a private school to join the Army. A disappointment to his dad. But he hated the regime, the corruption, the back-slapping, the boys-own mentality it all led to. Several times he'd almost mentioned it to Drake, but secretly enjoyed the one-upmanship it gave him over the Yorkshireman—even if he was the only one that knew it. The Army had made him, molded him, and given him real purpose.

Recently, since the Odin affair, Dahl had been wavering a little. The SPEAR missions were so deadly, so potentially lethal, but also among the most important that any team anywhere in the world were running right now.

But family came first.

Could he manage the best of both worlds? Possibly, but the sheer risk endemic in their missions and the power of their enemies made him wonder time and again what young Isabella and Julia would do if they heard their mad daddy had died.

He couldn't do it to them. But the missions kept coming. Each more crucial than the last. And now there was talk of Pandora and a new order and, beyond that, the greatest most immeasurable discovery of the ages.

Dahl breathed in. Time to stop relaxing and get his mind back on mission. It was best to confront these things at the right time, a time that was clearly not now. He would store it and move on. Johanna and the kids were already in DC. Maybe a trip to the White House was in order.

Then he thought better of it. With his track record in impulsiveness, walking around one of the most heavily guarded buildings in the world with your wife and kids in tow probably wasn't the smartest thing to do.

Disney then, he thought. What could possibly go wrong in a land of mice and ducks, pirates and princesses, cars and planes?

He wondered if the guy that played Goofy had ever experienced a half-nelson.

CHAPTER TWENTY FOUR

Karin Blake tapped away at her keyboard like a turbo-charged woodpecker; at first struggling to give the job her full attention, but gradually slipping into that geek power mode she loved. The brainwaves were surging, the ideas flicking and flashing like a firework show. Very quickly the screen and the cyber world became her only focus.

Komodo interrupted only occasionally. "How does this expert of theirs carry around a computer powerful enough to take this one on?"

Karin glanced up. The workstation she'd been presented with consisted of several hard-drives, wraparound screens and split-screening. It practically hummed a hacker's melody. She shrugged. "You can build a performance PC these days with a relatively small footprint, thanks to new ranges like the Mini-ITX motherboard. The liquid cooling solutions are nothing short of dramatic. An ultimate hacker's rig can be easily disguised as a suitcase. It's ugly but perfect."

"Gotcha. But how do they get so good, these cyber geeks?"

"Could be a hundred ways. Most likely is that he's ex-government. Did you know that DARPA built a mini-internet of their own a few years ago? A virtual internet as a test bed for cyberwarfare. They simulated different attack scenarios and came up with new defenses."

"Didn't DARPA create the Internet in the '60s?"

"Yes. So just imagine what they're up to now."

"So this guy is one of those?"

Karin shrugged. "I don't know. They were called 'cyberwarriors'. I guess I could ask him."

"You two are just gonna—schmooze."

"Not really. This is war. This is *my* fight." Karin clicked her fingers. "Circuit Girl is back in action. I may not wear a flak jacket or fire a Glock, but I have a hard drive and I'm damn willing to use it."

"How ya gonna get in there without him noticing?"

"Unlikely that I will. First, we learn the battlefield. Then, we employ methods on infiltration. Then it's attack or a covert op, exfiltration, and killing the bastard's foothold."

Karin pointed at the screen. "The objective is to disable him. Shut his grid down. Then, our soldiers in the field can act. We'll do a 'Pearl Harbor' on him since I don't have a virus at hand."

"A Pearl Harbor?"

"Hacker phrase named after . . . well, you know what it's named after, T-vor. It's a massive cyberattack on one or many computers, leading to infiltration then sabotage. We'll take him right out of the game."

Komodo squeezed her shoulder. Karin watched his face in the reflection of her screen, enjoying the slight smile that rested there. This was just what she needed.

"Did you know?" she said as she tapped and rolled her chair from screen to screen, stopping occasionally to sip coffee, keeping all the progressing information ticking over in her mind. "Cyberwarfare and cyberterrorism are now considered as much an act of war as the real thing. Every major defense agency is hiring teams of cyberwarriors. MI6 recently infiltrated an Al Qaeda website and replaced the recipe for a pipe bomb with a recipe for making cupcakes." She laughed. "Strange but true."

"A growing enterprise," Komodo noted.

"Everyone is conducting cyberwar games these days," Karin said. "Banks. Energy companies. Countries. Retailers and gaming firms. Social media organizations."

"What's that?" Komodo pointed at one of the screens, toward a newly emerging pulsing yellow ball of energy.

"That's him," Karin breathed. "I figured he had to be wireless. No hard-wiring in the field. Just a matter of casting the net and locating the signal with the cleverest arrangement of protocols. There's only one. And it's got more firewalls than Vesuvius in its heyday. Here goes."

She tapped and weaved steadily, finessing the connection as much with her body as her mind. Slinking over to a master hacker's subnet wasn't exactly easy, but if he responded like any other good hacker then, at first, he should monitor and watch the penetration, probably hoping he could infiltrate the infiltrator and hide inside her own systems. Karin had already employed a deceive program, which deployed multiple fake systems that the hacker might waste time seeking out. It was all just a ploy to gain enough time to shut the bastard right down.

Karin couldn't be too careful. Whilst she'd been out of the hacking game for some time now, her old signature—her method of operating—might still be recognized by a select few, and subsequently lead right back to her. If a master hacker knew your identity he'd have a better chance of defeating you in the cyber-theater of warfare. The militarization of cyberspace was not exclusive to governments and powerful organizations; it was still in the steady hands of the geek.

If the hacker detected her, his options were many and varied. Confusion. Surprise. Deception. Stimulation. Blockading. All viable options to effectively handle a penetration. Karin launched her probe, sitting back slightly, pausing to see what would happen.

Nothing at first. Her fists clenched. Her heart raced. This was the heart of the battle. Was he holding back, toying with her? Was he on the attack, about to launch? Was he investigating?

Now that she was in, it was time to attack. No covert soft option here. She played a concerto across her keyboard, effectively bringing up her prey's system, and began a search that would show her his security protocols. To take down his CCTV operation plus his cell and hardline monitoring capabilities, she'd need the heart of the system.

As she worked, the screen to her right blinked. It flashed, it went dark, and then suddenly resumed, only now it displayed the head and shoulders of a rather angry looking man.

Karin gawped. "Christ, how did he do that? And shit, I know him!"

Komodo blinked. "Huh?"

"I know this guy. Salami Bob, called SaBo for short. He was the guy helping Kovalenko in DC. The one that hacked the traffic light network. He also used to be a cyberwar strategist working for DARPA. Shit, I think I just met my match."

SaBo was indicating that Karin establish a communications link. With a few taps she did just that, then sat back chewing her lips as Sabo spoke.

"Good try, little miss. But I got you. I'm inside *you* now. You like?"

Komodo growled softly. "Say the word and this guy—"

"First strike." Karin waved the ex-Delta soldier away. "I drew first blood. Geek like you; all you can ever do is talk."

"Oh, I can do more than that."

SaBo's eyes flicked down as he entered a series of commands. Instantly, Karin's screen wavered, the image warping, but then righted itself as a red flashing band warned of an intruder alert.

"All right. You got firewalls." SaBo nodded. "Military grade at least." He made a face. "Gotta admit I *am* a little undersupplied out here but you gotta make do. Especially with the big bucks they're paying. Wanna join me, sweetheart? There's plenty of Sabo to go around."

Karin didn't react, casually playing for time. What SaBo didn't know was that she'd allowed for this. Her backup plan was actually superior to her original one.

"How much?" She played for time as she suspected he was doing.

"Watcha worth?"

Karin saw an intruder alert flash across the screen. SaBo was in their system. With a keystroke she wiped him out, denying access. He was gone in an instant. If he'd hung around a few moments longer she might even have been able to launch a denial-of-service attack; an attempt to make his machine and network unavailable to him.

"Straight out of the playbook," she scoffed. But she knew the playbook was a *living* document, constantly updated and improved upon.

Sabo grimaced, shoulders shuffling as his fingers moved furiously. He was planning something, of that Karin had no doubt; his lesser attacks were mere red herrings.

"Playbook?" The mere insinuation seemed to infuriate him.

But she was almost ready. Karin felt a moment of pride, a gathering of excitement, and pressed the button that would launch her epic, destructive counter attack. Many years ago, whilst immersed in this grand game of cyberstrategy, she'd developed her own virus; a program that carried one hell of a destructive payload. She'd never intended to use it—seeing the creation of such malware as a challenge more than anything. To keep it safe and secure, and away from thieving fingers, she'd hidden it inside a mostly redundant network. The virus had lain there, dormant, all these years, just awaiting activation.

Karin could think of no better time for it than now—an unstoppable attack that would wipe SaBo out for good.

It took a second for the old network to respond, a while for those old circuits to start whirring, but when they did Karin's virus shot across the web at lightning speed.

CHAPTER TWENTY FIVE

Drake led the way as the team pounded toward the location of the closest nano-vest and the unfortunate person Coyote and her mercs had forced into it.

The appearance of the green signals alongside their own red ones had galvanized them all into action. If any doubts remained as to Coyote's iniquity—especially within Drake—they had now departed. The stretch between sugary Shelly Cohen and merciless Coyote was still a tough one, but it was becoming easier to make. All those years, all that time laboring in the field, isolated, sometimes under fire, never knowing if they were going to make it out; the only thing his men and himself could look forward to were those homely, sweet tones at the end of the day. Shelly had pulled more than one man home through with the sheer charm and reassurance she offered.

At the same time she'd secretly been plotting her next kill.

What type of person could do that?

Drake shrugged it off as they raced up the final steep hill toward the graveyard. Dahl was staring intently at his screen, pinpointing the closest green-colored signal. Mai and Alicia led the way, keeping lookout but moving fast, hyperaware that Coyote had given them only two hours to defuse four bombs. Up into the graveyard they hurried. Drake slowed as a hundred timeworn, dilapidated gravestones appeared, some standard designs, others crafted into many different shapes and sizes.

He turned to Dahl. "C'mon mate. You got a position?"

"It's not that accurate." Dahl pointed ahead. "There."

They aimed at a cross-section of paths, beyond which lay a flat, sparser area of ground. Drake was the first to see the partially filled shallow grave . . .

. . . and the coffin that sat inside.

"No." He gasped in horror. "Oh no."

Mai came to a sudden stop. "They buried him alive?"

Alicia raced through and jumped straight down into the grave. "No time to fuck about. Help me!"

Alicia wrenched at the lid of the coffin. The earth beneath her feet, which ended just below the lid, hampered her movements. Drake saw immediately that the thing had been nailed shut with some heavy duty fixings.

"Jump in," he cried. "Shit. Just everyone get in there."

The team hurled themselves into the open grave, trying to get a decent handhold, and straining their muscles until the lid squealed. There was no thought as to whether the lid might be booby trapped, no thought as to whether or not a sniper was watching. The man in the coffin was dying in more ways than one; the team's ethics put him first.

Drake felt small splinters jab at his fingers, slicing under his nails. He gripped harder. Maybe they would give him better leverage. He wrenched again and again, grunting with the effort. Dahl scooped out a mound of earth with his shovel hands then leaned back, pushing himself into the ground. Then, after setting himself, he kicked hard at the lid.

Bit by bit, against the wishes of its tough squealing fixings, the lid came up.

Now with space to work, the team dipped their shoulders and heaved. Drake immediately saw the man trapped inside, a duct-tape gag across his mouth, hands tied in front of him. The eyes said it all—they said, "Look out! *Look out!*"

Drake held his palm out. "Don't worry. We know you're wired and we brought an expert."

He looked up. Alicia's eyes were slits, as if to say, "Oh yeah?" Mai frowned. Dahl assumed Drake meant him and started blowing expertly on his hands.

Drake smiled. "Not you. Him." He pointed.

The slightly belabored figure of Michael Crouch had just entered the graveyard.

"Christ," Alicia whispered. "I forgot about him. Did ya get lost, old man?"

Crouch toiled up and then leaned over, breathing heavily. He held up a finger for three seconds, then straightened and stared at Alicia. "Fuck you."

Drake hid a smile. Crouch may be the big boss, the biggest in fact, but coming up through the ranks meant he shared the soldiers' camaraderie. He was one of them. Accepted. He turned again to the bound man. "Where's the vest?"

Dahl shook his head. "Luckily I'm not a dumb Northerner," he said as he worked. "An education can sometimes come in handy." He peeled the duct tape from the man's mouth. "That should help."

Drake was about to retort, but Crouch stopped him. Still panting a little, he dropped down into the coffin and leaned over the man. After a second he lifted his tied hands up and pulled the shirt from his trousers.

"Not a vest as such," he said. "More a belt."

Drake moved around to get a better look. Alicia called out that twenty minutes had already passed. Although this man was the relatively lucky one of the four—he was their first—time would now count down at an exponential rate, increasing the pressure with each tick of the clock.

"Can it be defused?" Dahl wondered.

"Of course. It's essentially an explosive vest," Crouch said. "It's the *nano* side of things that worries me."

Drake had heard of nanotechnology but knew only the basics. "You mean, why use nano explosives when C4 is so much easier to find?"

"Exactly."

Mai spoke up. "This isn't something we can investigate right now," she said. "We're at the heart of a tournament. Cut off from the rest of the world and stuck in this unlucky town. Can you defuse the vest or not?"

Crouch glanced around at her then held the vest up in his hand, letting it dangle toward the ground. "Yes, Mai. I can."

Mai looked surprised. Dahl smiled. Alicia clapped like an overexcited seal. "Man can't run for shit, but slip a bomb into a man's pants and Mr. Crouch is all over it."

Crouch handed the belt off to Drake then turned to help the prisoner up. "Do you people have to put up with her *all* the time?"

Drake stared intently at the vest-cum-belt. "Yeah. Except when she's off shagging someone's boss. Usually her own."

Alicia leaned over to help Crouch. "Seriously, what the hell did you do?"

Crouch shrugged. "Removed the electrical detonator, staying wary of static sparks, of course."

Alicia nodded wisely. "Of course."

"Contrary to what the movie makers would have us believe all you have to do is remove the detonator or timer that controls the bomb. It's not terribly complicated but I guess doesn't make for good ratings."

Dahl suddenly shook the tracking device to get everyone's attention. "Let's move, guys. We still have three more to deactivate."

Mai studied the trees. "And I just wonder at which one we'll finally meet Coyote."

Drake shared her sentiment. "It's been a long time coming."

Crouch joined them, having untied the prisoner, directed him toward the open church doors and instructed him not to try to escape the town. "The British forces will be massing outside," he said. "Readying a full-scale assault. We have to hurry. This town's going to become a battlefield and no mistake."

Dahl shook the tracking device. "Ten minutes to the next vest, I think."

They moved off. Crouch reached for the nano-vest that Drake carried. It was the shape of a normal belt, but wider and with a plastic buckle. Made of leather, the vest had loops that helped it fit snugly over the shoulders and was extremely flat, so that it left no tell-tale bulges.

"Incredible," he said. "Our enemies would love to get their hands on this shit."

Dahl said, "I guess nanotechnology is the same as any other kind of technology. Helpful to humankind until some maniac thinks of a way to exploit its potential for war and personal gain."

"Nano-thermite—the explosive—is a cutting edge nano-particulate mix of aluminum and ferric oxide. The key is the extremely small particle size. They have more surface area in contact with the particles of the different chemicals that make up the explosive. After a reaction is initiated this greater surface area causes a faster rate of reaction, making for a more powerful outcome. And by making these things at the nanoscale engineers can actually custom design *each* explosive, enabling them to manufacture the perfect application for any desired event."

Mai shook her head. "That's crazy."

"Conspiracy theories abound regarding nano-thermite," Crouch went on. "The biggest of which, of course, is the twin towers. The photograph that shows the top of the towers starting to crumble—that's a nano-explosion. The rate of collapse bears more similarities with a nano-blast than anything that might be caused by a plane." He shrugged. "But that's all theory, of course. We live in the real world, and we know that the *unknown* happens every day. Every hour. What appears to be real might in fact be a clever illusion and what appears to be false can in fact be true, just an unknown coalescence of unfamiliar reactions. Any man that disputes that is a fool."

Drake drew him back to the vest as they hurried along. "So why that?"

"Seriously, I have no idea. Obviously, it's custom made. It has a purpose. An engineer built this vest from a careful design, and that design, in my experience at least, was envisioned by his boss."

"Is this nano-thermite hard to get hold of?" Mai asked.

"Almost impossible," Crouch confirmed. "Outside of high-ranking military personnel with appropriate security credentials and the like."

"So somebody has an agenda," Drake said. "And this is maybe just the start? I mean, it can't have been manufactured only to be used in Sunnyvale, surely."

"Agreed." Crouch said. "Nanotechnology is high stakes. World stakes."

Alicia had been twisting her head in a complicated movement, trying to scrutinize the vest. "So where are these bloody explosives? All I see is a leather belt."

"That's the idea, dear." Crouch gave her a devious smile. "Nano-thermite explosives are manufactured and modified on a micro scale. You certainly can't see them."

"So they're inside the belt." Alicia let the 'dear' comment slide. This time.

"Assuredly so."

Alicia slowed as Dahl held up a hand. She dropped her voice to a whisper. "Why don't terrorists use this kinda technology then?"

Crouch breathed slowly. "They don't have access to it . . . so far. The devil with staying ahead of our would-be murderers is that we have to be *several* steps ahead. The technology that *beats* nano-weapons also has to be realized. Recently, through nanotechnology, a liquid was developed that can totally neutralize explosive substances the kind of which the shoebomber tried to use. It can be sprayed on. All airports should carry this by now. Do you see?"

"It never ends," Alicia said. "I see that."

Drake agreed. "Long after we're dead and gone there'll be others out there saving the world. Because for as long as there are good men striving to use their skills to help advance the world, there'll be schemers, cheats and fanatics that want to own it."

Dahl hissed for silence. Drake glanced over the Swede's shoulder and saw that the flashing green signal put their next tormented civilian in the middle of a building under construction. It was a two-story affair, narrow and only two-thirds built, still with scaffolding on the inside and out, and with window and door frames open to the elements. A concrete mixer and rubble-filled skip stood in the front yard. Through the gaps Drake discerned various odd shapes, now becoming clearer as the dawn started to rise. In the surrounding houses people were starting to stir, some oblivious to the night's events, others wise and staying low.

Very soon, a reckoning would be reached.

Dahl pointed through the gap where the front door would be. "Just a few feet down the hallway," he said, "is my closest estimate."

Drake led the way, closely followed by Mai. When they passed the area indicated by the flashing dot, Dahl called out to them. When they passed it again, still seeing nothing, the Swede shook his head.

"I don't get it."

Drake surveyed the hallway. It was wide and high, with plasterboard to both sides. Empty doorways provided dark outlets further away. The ceiling was an untidy jumble of exposed timbers and hanging wires. Again, Dahl called out as they passed the correct location.

Drake let out a breath. "There's nothing here but floors and walls, Dahl. Is your equipment malfunctioning?"

Dahl lowered the tracking device. "Floor and walls? Oh shit, remember the grave?"

Drake caught on in the blink of an eye. Instantly, he turned and kicked at the plasterboard, his boot cracking the gypsum and going straight through. He pulled out a chunk with his hands, ignored the white plume, and kept going. To his side Mai attacked another eight-by-four sheet and Alicia another. Gypsum dust filled the air, making them cough. Mai curled one hand around a jagged hole beside her head and pulled hard. The piece came away, leaving her staring into the frightened eyes of another victim.

"Here."

Crouch galloped over. He ignored the man's silent pleas whilst checking under his shirt. "Same layout as before," he reported. "Give me a minute."

"Not too long," Dahl said. "We've taken over one hour to deactivate the first two. Even for a Swedish elite soldier that's not a good start."

Drake pretended to choke on plasterboard dust, coughing, "Swedish elite soldier," as he fell to his knees, head down. Dahl threw a black look his way.

Crouch unhooked the nano-vest, holding it up to the light. Mai let the leather feed through her fingers.

"Same as the last one. Exactly."

Alicia pursed her lips. "So. Did someone have a surplus of these things and sell them to the highest bidder?"

"Coyote?" Crouch sounded doubtful.

"The Blood King," Alicia stressed. "This is his final curtain call."

"Perhaps. But the op is still Coyote's. She'd have full autonomy. And the nano angle just doesn't make sense."

"Well, if we can stop the debate and get moving," Dahl said. "We might even be able to save the other two. Then you can examine the vests all you like."

The group prepared to move off, directing the civilian again toward the church. They didn't want him going home, pointing out that he'd already been abducted once tonight. The church might be the safest place.

Dahl held up the tracking device. "All right folks—"

The streak hit him in the midriff, travelling at high speed and taking no prisoners. Dahl's exclamation of shock was torn from his mouth. The tracking device flew into the air. The Swede flew back and slammed into the side wall, shattering apart even more plasterboard and landing in a heap, spluttering.

A darkness detached itself from his body, a lithe, twisting darkness, every sinuous movement speaking of malice.

It leapt at Alicia, making the Englishwoman squeal before she could catch herself. The attack was so sudden, so precise and hard, that it had disconcerted everyone. The single person in the team that wouldn't have been disquieted was Dahl, and he'd been taken out first.

Design.

Drake ran to Alicia's aid. His friend had recovered quickly, but the bruise along the top of her left eye was already coloring. She stumbled away, and Drake was in. The Yorkshireman stepped up hard, striking at the black-clad figure with tough, accurate blows. As he worked, Mai drifted in from the right-hand side.

"Beauregard Alain," she said softly. "Try me. I'd like to take you one-on-one."

Soft laughter issued from beneath the mask. No words, just the whispered sibilance. No arrogant return, only quiet confidence. Drake knew that kind of confidence and knew better than to push the kind of man that oozed it. They needed to take this enemy down, and fast. He struck even harder, but the Frenchman had other ideas. With a lightning quick rib kick he doubled Drake over and switched his attention toward Mai.

The ex-ninja targeted the man's knee with a side kick, his throat with a finger jab and his ribs with a flying-knee—all in the same movement. Beauregard caught them all and executed a comeback of his own. As Mai drifted past, he elbow-jabbed and back-kicked, striking flesh, then whirled with a reverse flying kick. The blow glanced across Mai's skull, barely making contact.

Dahl groaned, trying to extricate himself from the wall and the broken plasterboard and failing. Crouch had already retrieved the tracking device and was checking to make sure it was still working. Drake and Alicia had recovered and were looking for the best way to enter the fray.

Beauregard's head swiveled from side to side, the movement inside the mask giving him the appearance of a deadly predator; a black snake, a confident killer. Then he performed a feat Drake wasn't even sure Mai could pull off. He leapt straight up, pushed off the wall at his back, and smashed both feet into Mai's chest, using her as a way of deflecting his flight toward Drake and Alicia. Then, still in mid-air, he kicked Drake hard in the chin and Alicia right on the nose. He landed with a flourish.

And rose with a semi-automatic in each hand. "Seems I won," he said with a heavy accent but no bravado in his voice.

Before he could fire, Michael Crouch moved to stand in front of the stunned team. "Not so fast," he said. "You'll have to go through me first."

"And you are?"

But the hesitation was clear. The fact that he hadn't pulled the trigger was obvious. He knew this man.

"You know me, Beauregard. And I know you. We worked together, before you became greedy and went rogue. You were a good man back then. Fact is—" Crouch coughed. "I still am."

Beauregard still waited. The gun didn't waver a millimeter. He seemed to be weighing up past impressions with current positions. Clearly, there were a lot of factors involved, both old and new.

"Who are you working for, Beauregard?" Crouch suddenly asked. "What do you know of the nano-vests?"

All of a sudden Beauregard moved. His gun arm flexed. Quickly, he saluted Crouch with the weapon. "For the past," he said thickly. "One reprieve. Next time, it will go differently, Mr. Crouch. Do not get in my way again."

Then he was gone, a shadow blending with the retreating dark of the night. A ghost warrior, flitting beyond vision.

"Shit and bollocks." Alicia slapped Crouch on the back. "You do have some uses, old man."

Crouch nodded. "Once this is all over we'll need to move fast. Beauregard is yet another deep mystery. The man wouldn't stoop so low as to enter a tournament like this. Somebody is running him, a hidden party. Add Mossad and the nano-vests, and you'll see that we need to finish this fast, then get back to MI6 to get the war cabinet involved. If James isn't awake yet I'll bloody well shake his head from his shoulders. The security of much more than a small English village is at stake."

Drake knew that Crouch was referring to the British Prime Minister, James Ronson, without hint or thought of vanity. Crouch was simply the most well-connected man he knew, and for good reason. If he wanted to he could topple governments and move mountains. In fact, Drake imagined, with the Ninth Division now defunct, Crouch could pretty much write his own ticket.

What next for the eminent leader?

Dahl had managed to climb upright and dust off. He retrieved the tracker from Crouch. "Now then. After that—short interlude—we can continue. Only thirty minutes left to rescue two people. Only one tracker. Are we ready?"

Drake nodded, still reeling a little. "Stop yer jabbering and move!"

CHAPTER TWENTY SIX

The third flashing signal came from over near the supermarket. Drake hightailed it that way, bruises aching, self-esteem more than a little bit battered.

"If we see that bastard again," he said. "We need to take him down hard."

Mai rubbed the top of her chest. "I believe I underestimated him. Being French and all."

"C'mon Little Sprite!" Alicia barked. "What are you? A *country* racist? Russians are bad because nothing works right. Frenchmen in tights are weak because they're, well, French. Wow."

Drake shook his head. "I shoulda known, after all that just happened, you would mention the tights."

"What?" Alicia said innocently. "I mean they were rather *tight*. And that sexy high-kick near my face put his—"

"No." Drake put his head in his hands. "Please no."

"Oh yeah. He did it to you too, didn't he?"

Drake saw the supermarket up ahead and pointed with blessed relief. "How's the signal, Dahl?"

The Swede estimated the distances. "Puts our man inside the damn supermarket."

They hurried along as time ticked away. Twenty five minutes remained until Coyote's deadline. Drake entered through the broken window and glanced around at the damage they'd already helped cause.

"Cops are going to have fun with this in a day or two."

"Don't worry about it," Crouch advised. "Cops are the least of *our* worries."

Dahl followed his tracking device, at last coming up against the rear wall. "Damn. Just another bloody wall. What is it with this thing?"

Drake tested the construction. "Well, they can't have put someone behind this thing and sealed it up again so fast," he said. "Feels sturdy."

"Wait." Mai was moving along the wall. "Here."

Drake paced to her side. "Coyote's men are indeed bastards," he said. "As if we needed more convincing."

A heavy metal door stood before them, featureless except for a handle and vision panel. Nobody needed to be told this was the supermarket's storage freezer. One glance inside confirmed a woman lying prone on the floor, hands and feet bound. When Drake knocked she didn't move to acknowledge them.

"How the hell do we get in?" Alicia asked.

Drake eyed the nano-vests Crouch carried. "What about one of those?"

The Ninth Division man frowned. "Could kill the woman inside. And us. Could bring down the entire building."

"Bollocks."

"Wait." Dahl stepped up and peered inside. "How far away is she from the door?" He stepped back. "Could work."

"What?" Drake asked. *"What* could work?"

Dahl ran at a sprint through the supermarket and out the broken windows.

Drake looked around at his companions, face to face. "I really don't like it when he gets an idea in his head."

"Yeah," Alicia said. "Forget the nano explosions. Here comes Torsten Dahl."

And here he did come, at the wheel of a Toyota Hilux, teeth gritted and face set through the windshield, gunning the engine for all it was worth. The large vehicle smashed through the already demolished windows, shattering what glass and framework remained, then ploughed through the fallen shelves and piles of groceries. Drake and the team scattered. Dahl hung on grimly. Box displays and large baskets full of crisps and biscuits were destroyed, slithering under the wheels and smashing to left and right. The truck bounced, yawing over a pile of groceries. On an angle, the front bars struck the freezer door, pushing it back and shattering the frame. The

Hilux came to a stop halfway through, and Dahl revved hard, slamming the vehicle into reverse.

"Fuck!"

Drake and the others, on their way forward, suddenly had to dive out of the way again.

Dahl burned rubber as he reversed fast, taking most of the door with him and smashing even more of the supermarket to pieces. Once the front wheels were clear, Drake ran again, this time bouncing from pile to pile and into the demolished freezer. He dropped to his knees beside the trapped woman.

Rolled her over. The eyes fluttered softly, the breathing shallow. He nodded at Crouch. "Do it."

He watched the man disarm the ignition mechanism. In truth, now that he'd seen it done there was nothing to it. A simple matter of disengaging a wire and a metal plate. But if Crouch hadn't been around . . . the results might have been much different.

If Crouch hadn't been around . . .

The thought gave birth to a deeper consideration. *Did Coyote quietly control Crouch's presence in order to help with the vests? In order to realize their wider potential and see what might be coming?*

But he was giving the woman too much respect, yet again. For some reason Shelly Cohen would just not transmogrify into the terrible mien of Coyote that he held in his mind. The match wouldn't fit.

Crouch held up the vest. "Done."

"Now, fast." Dahl stepped down from the Hilux. "Number four is only at the village square, just a few minutes away. We have twenty minutes."

"The center of town." Drake nodded. "Sounds crafty and sly to me. This is the one, guys. Coyote's final play. Dial in your best game and turn it up to A."

Alicia was already moving. "Dude, that's my *only* game."

CHAPTER TWENTY SEVEN

Karin played a game of digital warfare against the great and notorious SaBo, only the risks and rewards involved were far beyond any 'game'. They were life-threatening.

Time and again she breached his system, only to be routed out. Komodo kept her going with coffee and Mountain Dew. When his eyes started to glaze over from trying to keep track of the scrolling code, keywords and flashing warning signals, he wandered over to a second bank of computer terminals where a man wearing an army uniform sat at ease.

"How ya doin'?"

"Good." The man he knew as Sergeant Pearson gave him a perfunctory smile. "Feeling a little undermanned at this moment. But otherwise okay."

"Undermanned?" Komodo asked. Nobody had said anything about being undermanned.

"Budget cuts. Recession. We're two men down twenty four hours a day. Add that up, sir, and that's a lot of slack."

"Damn straight." Komodo nodded at the door. "How safe is this place?"

"Well, it's not Tesco, sir, but it certainly isn't MI6 either."

Komodo grunted at the lack of real information. "Bud, we ain't exactly got a great track record when it comes to safe houses. If there's someone you can call I'd do it now."

The ex-Delta man walked away, returning to Karin's side.

"Sir," the man called from behind. "This isn't a safe house. It's a joint government-private sector run building. We just rent the basement."

Komodo just stared. "Then call someone."

Karin glanced around at him. "What's all that about, T-vor?"

"Nothing special," he said. "How you doin'?"

"Wins and losses," she said. "Nothing vital. SaBo's reputation is well-deserved. It's a dance, like combat, only we don't get hurt like you do."

Komodo grumbled. "I never felt combat was much like a dance."

"You know what I mean. Look . . ." She tapped a button, executing a command. The picture flashed across immediately to the screen to her right, tracking the progress of her latest attack, showing circuits penetrated and firewalls breached. Several layers disappeared like confetti on the breeze, destroyed, but then a flashing grid-barrier stopped them and a net enveloped Karin's point of infiltration. All of a sudden the screen went blank.

Karin sighed. "And another attack is thwarted."

"What about your secret weapon?"

Karin smiled. "Worming its way through a myriad of redundant circuits. It is most definitely the key to beating SaBo. I just have to keep him busy until it gets to where I need it to be."

"Got it."

The room's single door swung open. Komodo, still thinking of Sergeant Pearson's words, swung around with a hand hovering over his holstered weapon. A Glock was all they would let him keep, and that only as a courtesy. To Komodo, it felt a little like brandishing a lollipop, but he knew the effect would be somewhat different.

Now, however, only Pearson came into sight. "We just received an update from the field," he reported. "Our forces have assembled at Sunnyvale. The SAS are there, coordinating with elements of the British Army, Hostage Rescue, what was SO13 and SO12, now SO15, and CO19 along with the Special Projects Unit, which had actually been formed to combat hit men, or assassins, and several units of special police are ready to move. Hardware is on the ground and in the air. A full-scale assault will begin within the hour."

Karin bit her lip. "They are aware of the merc army, yes?"

Pearson nodded. "We have civilians already in extreme danger. Their safety is the prime concern. The Prime Minister and COBRA have signed off on it. They're going in, Miss."

Karin nodded, her eyes betraying her concern. Not only for her friends but for everyone involved. An assault would leave many dead. But if she could just defeat SaBo in time, she might be able to help save lives.

In her distress, apprehension and determination she failed to notice that one of SaBo's lesser signals had breached the tiniest part of her system. It would feed him nothing, give him no upper hand in their cyberbattle.

But if he piggybacked a cell signal onto it he would instantly have their location.

CHAPTER TWENTY EIGHT

Drake raced out of the supermarket, hitting the concrete running. The team pounded along at his side, Crouch already falling back. After only a minute's sprint he pulled up short.

"Wait!"

Everyone reined it in around him. He held up a finger. "Listen."

The unmistakable sound of military choppers, of military might, and even the sound of a gathering force drifted on the breeze and beat a rhythm through the clouds. Drake made a face.

"That is more than a slow assembly, my friends. That is the sound of a military force getting ready to strike."

"You're right." Crouch nodded as he finally lumbered up. "But they have to wait. They *need* to wait. Not just because they don't know about the nano-vests, but because of their *presence*. What else could Coyote have up her damn sleeve?"

Drake pointed to the rear of the supermarket. "You did it once, sir. Time to go again."

Crouch nodded. "Agreed. Oh, and Drake? I already told you I am no longer anyone's boss. So stop calling me sir. Crouch will do. Or Michael."

"Mick?" Alicia piped up. "Mickey? Miks? Oh, I like that."

Crouch glared into her face. "Keep on talking, Myles, and I'll be happy to blacken your other eye. No charge."

Alicia turned away. The black eye was a matter of pride. Or rather—injured pride. She glared at the town. "Shouldn't we be going?"

The four SPEAR team members approached Sunnyvale's town square with extreme caution. The area was an open grid, lined with thick stone pavers and bordered by a waist-height stone wall. Several gaps in the wall provided entrances, each one marked by twin ornate posts. Above it all a pitched tiled roof provided shelter, held up by thick wooden columns. Flanking the square itself were two rows of stores and cafes, a large dilapidated-looking hotel with a 'Closed for Refurbishment' sign across the door and other businesses, a road leading toward the castle, and another leading out of town. A reddish light lit the skies above the square, casting a ruddy, almost fiery glow over the entire scene.

Nothing moved; not an early riser nor even an inquisitive bird. No sounds intruded upon the deep blanket of silence.

But a dozen men stood inside the town square. And another dozen stood around the outside.

And one smaller figure stood before them all. Revealed at last for all that she truly was.

Shelly Cohen.

The Coyote.

CHAPTER TWENTY NINE

Drake saw no value in sticking to the shadows. He walked straight out into the middle of the road and toward Coyote.

Life obviously continued during those next few minutes. Seconds passed. Minutes blurred. Men and women loved and cried and died. Governments plotted. Young children dreamed of being Elsa or Anna, as most young children did in those days. The whole world kept on turning.

Matt Drake stopped not ten feet from the Coyote.

"You have been on my mind, Matt Drake." The sugary tones hadn't changed. "And I know—dumb of me to keep up that kind of connection. But sharp of me to focus on my worst enemy."

Drake stared, trying not to let his mouth drop open. Even after all this, after everything he now knew, he still imagined someone else might pop out and start up some kind of manic laughter. It couldn't be Shelly . . . could it?

"I don't get it," he said honestly.

Shelly shrugged, her long, dark hair falling across one tanned cheek. "Imagine my surprise then. When I found out I was a closet psychopath and somehow needed to vent the urge. Every—" she shrugged again, "couple of weeks."

Drake sensed his team coming up behind. "What does that mean? You 'found out' you were a psychopath."

"It's not something they tell your parents when you're born, Matt. Not written on your birth certificate. You figure it out. More pleasure is gained from performing one act than another. The trick is—harnessing it."

Drake closed his eyes. "I've been looking for you for years."

"I've followed your trail," Coyote said. "You know you gotta stay frisky. Maybe after this, you can let it go."

"You murdered my wife, and . . . and—"

What would she do? Deny it? Say—"I know" and fuel his wrath? Apologize?

But Shelly Cohen just stared at him, blank expression betraying no emotion.

"And Michael?" Drake almost spat at her. "The Ninth?"

Coyote's gaze flicked away very briefly. "Only the second job of my career that I almost refused to do."

Drake guessed the first. "*Why?*"

"What? Coyote? It's my outlet and I enjoy it. Do I have regrets? Yes. Would I do things differently than I have? Yes. But, as you know Matt, to stay on top sometimes you have to do bad things."

"Like this?" Drake indicated the town around them. "Harming innocent people?"

"Kovalenko was very clear when he hired me. Carry out his wishes regarding you four and the rest of your annoying little team. And listen to the instructions of Tyler Webb."

Alicia shifted a little. "Who?"

Coyote said nothing, her eyes never leaving Drake.

"So here we stand," Drake said. "What's next? You gonna get your goons to mow us down in cold blood?"

"Personally, I'd like to gut every last one of you." Coyote licked her lips and smiled lasciviously. "And taste the blood. But, again, Kovalenko's orders were specific."

Drake heard the words coming out of her mouth. Like the rest of the Ninth boys he had known Shelly Cohen took on jobs of her own, but the sight of this cold-blooded, eager killer still grated on him. "How specific?"

"You four must fight and die." She smiled; the charming, monstrous host. "Last man standing. Remember?"

Drake looked around, now truly stumped. "And how the hell do you intend to make us do that?"

Coyote's smile now filled her full face. Even a small chuckle escaped those full red lips. "I thought you might wonder about that. Interesting dilemma, yes? What to do? I agonized for hours. Then I realized the answer was right under my nose."

Alicia leaned forward. "You ain't coming anywhere near me with those filthy lips, love."

Coyote pouted. "Ah, the rest of the team. Alicia Myles—looking for a real home ever since Mom and Dad fell to pieces. Never found one. The black eye suits you, by the way. Rather symbolic of your journey through life. Mai Kitano—so much potential yet so badly broken. Torsten Dahl—not much to say. Dropped out of private school to join the Army. My main Intel on you consisted of just two words—'mad bastard'. You out of all of them I find interesting."

Drake never lost a single ounce of concentration. "And what of all the innocents, Shelly? Who cries for them?"

Coyote sighed. "Psychopaths don't have consciences, Matt. It's one of the perks."

"Look." Mai stepped up. "Why don't we just say we fought and I won? There's only going to be one winner here."

Drake looked askance at his girlfriend. "Only if you fight yourself."

Dahl stayed quiet, never the boastful one, except in banter.

Alicia coughed. "Thanks for the vote of confidence, bitch."

Coyote stood back, watching them. The playful smile never left her lips and the now bittersweet tones never altered. "It's good that you're ready."

Mai was staring at the rest of her team, genuinely surprised. "Am I missing something?"

Drake only had eyes for Coyote. "You're sick. Get help. Don't feed your infection into the lives of so many decent human beings."

Now Coyote's face hardened. "Decent? You have got to be kidding me. I only *ever* took the bad ones. The child killers. The molesters. The drug pushers. Kingpins. I only *ever* took the worst of the worst, the most capable opponents. But one thing you learn—the more jobs you take, the more you're in demand. And the more you're in demand, the less you can decline. There comes a point, a turning point, when it's stick or twist. You slowly decay—as in never pushing anything forward—or you move ahead. Test everything you think you know about yourself. Grow some balls and jump headlong into the arena. *That's* when you live. *That's* when you grow. *That's* when you become the person you were always meant to be. And Matt—" She paused.

And said sadly, "That was Alyson."

Drake felt his throat close up, the memories crashing down like killer waves. Time did not heal this kind of memory—he already knew that. The painful loss would be with him until his dying day. And Coyote just didn't *get it*. The woman was a self-confessed psycho. A born killer. If Drake had been hoping for a reason, a confession, even a sliver of remorse, he would not find it here. And the worse thing was—he believed Coyote *was* regretful in her own way, but feelings like regret, compassion and love were sentiments she just couldn't imagine.

There were no answers here. Nor would there ever be. In life's tribunal there were no real judgments, no major prosecutions. Just experience. And emotion.

"So here we stand," he said again. "What's next?"

"Where's Michael?" Coyote suddenly said, as if realizing for the first time that her old boss was missing.

Drake made a noncommittal gesture. "He didn't want to see you."

"Michael Crouch would never avoid a confrontation. Do not play me for a fool. Where is he?"

Drake drew a line slowly across his throat, undaunted by the firepower aimed at him. "Time's almost up, Shelly. Make your play."

Dahl surreptitiously tapped the tracking device still clasped in one hand. "Number four's time is almost up. Do something, Drake, or I will."

"Location?"

"The hotel." Dahl was referencing the tall, wide structure to their left which took up a good chunk of the main street.

Coyote stepped forward, reducing the distance between her and Drake to a daring few yards. "You want my play? Well here it is! I knew there was only one thing that would make goody-goodies like you people fight. And here they are!"

Drake experienced a foreign emotion right then—nerves. *What the hell can she possibly mean? To what depths has Shelly Cohen sunk?*

Then he found out. And felt something die inside.

Coyote's mercs parted and allowed twelve civilians to be marched through their ranks. Every single one of them wore a nano-vest.

Coyote snarled at Drake. "Fight to the death or they die. Fight or watch them explode. And all the rest of these pathetic townspeople. I know where they hide, where they cower in fear. I will burn them in their churches. I will destroy their homes. I will send them to their precious heavens with a rocket and a bullet in their backs. Them, and their precious children."

Drake felt his heart lurch even as adrenalin electrified his entire body. "You crazy, crazy woman. What have you done?"

"She earned a pay packet," Dahl said. "Do it, Drake. Take the fight inside."

Drake nodded. "The hotel," he said. "It seems we have no choice. We will fight, but you will not win the day, Shelly. Nothing can save you now."

Coyote smiled back, sugary as ever. "The hotel is perfect. We have CCTV, of course. I want to see every blow, every broken bone. I want to live it with you, feel the pain and the exultation. And only one comes out alive. Or these cowards, and this town, dies."

Drake moved fast, crossing the sidewalk and hitting the hotel swing-doors as hard as he could. Inside, a huge entrance hall opened out and up, ending in an arched ceiling a hundred feet high. The reception desk appeared to be a mile away, across a set of thick Turkish carpets. Plush sofas, chaises longues, gleaming wooden desks and antique furnishings filled the room, interrupted randomly by several out-of-place, mock-Egyptian relics—a sarcophagus, a sphinx and a scarab clinging to the wall. Mirrors were everywhere, an attempt to make the outsize hall seem even larger than it was. To the right a bank of elevators stood waiting. To the left a curving staircase led to higher floors.

Drake spotted the fourth man easily, strapped to the underside of a table.

"Thirty seconds!" Dahl cried. "Give or take!"

Drake launched himself, sliding the last few feet on his knees. "*Give or take?*"

"Calm down." Alicia was at his side. "No need to squeak about it."

Mai came in from the left. "Yeah. We've faced worse than this."

Drake unclipped the belt and separated the metal plates. The entire process took eight seconds. Once safe, they freed the man and directed him toward the door. A minute ticked by as they watched him go.

Then Drake turned to Dahl. "I guess it's time to see who's best."

"Yeah. Sorry about the bruises."

Drake nodded. "Me too."

Alicia turned to face Mai. "Time for that rematch, Little Sprite?"

"If you're referring to that *scrap* we had on Waikiki Beach, Taz, I wouldn't get your hopes up. That was . . . recreation."

"And now you're serious?"

"Mostly."

Alicia spread her hands. "Then let's see, shall we?"

On all four fronts, the battle was met.

CHAPTER THIRTY

Karin heard the door open for the hundredth time that night. She heard the faint rustle as Komodo turned around. She heard the voice of Sergeant Pearson.

But this time it was different.

Low. Harsh. Crawling with concern. Quickly, she tore her gaze away from the computer screen and the point of SaBo's latest attack to listen.

"Now?" Komodo cried out. "Here?"

Pearson's answer was rushed. "As I said. We have no time. Arm yourself, man."

Karin felt her mouth go dry. It sounded like . . . like . . .

At that moment, Pearson's head blew apart. Red sprayed the wall beside him, dripping like melting hieroglyphics. The sergeant's body toppled through the door. Komodo caught it in time to whip the man's gun from his holster, taking his tally to two, and pulled out his extra clips. Before he could try anything else or even utter a word of warning, the door itself blasted open, slamming back against its hinges and the other wall.

The first protagonist barged in, getting tangled with Pearson's body and falling to one knee. Komodo stood calmly over him, firing one bullet into the back of his neck. The second was just behind. Komodo timed it to perfection, waiting for the exact moment in which to push-kick the open door closed on the man's onrushing face.

A scream signified success.

Komodo back off a little. He didn't want to fire through the gap, and give his enemy reason to shy away from their attack and start lobbing in some form of incendiary device. Karin kept silent as his training kicked in. She trusted him completely, and almost turned back to her computer work.

Then she wondered how these goons had found them.

Has to be . . . oh no! She scanned the screens, following each minute line of code and all the representative grid lines. And then she saw it. The faintest of pulsing lights, signifying a low signal. But something SaBo could use.

The bastard had beaten her.

Used her. Here, in her own back garden. Literally, the place she grew up. Where her parents had died. Where Ben had died.

She coughed hard, choked. She would never give in. she killed the signal and ignored SaBo's instant request for a chat. The hacker would want to gloat. Of course he would. Well, she could give him something to take his mind off cheap victory.

The virus was ready. It was in place, just awaiting the command.

Behind her, Komodo grunted heavily as a man landed on his back. This was in addition to the man already grappling him around the waist. The only reason they hadn't fired was their unwillingness to hit each other. A third waded in.

Karin quit her post and ran to her boyfriend's aid. Yes, as she knew from before, civilian martial arts training was tame compared to military training, but it was all she had to offer. And it held the element of surprise.

She struck hard and fast, jabbing the kidneys of the man holding Komodo's waist and the ribs of the one clinging to his back. Her side-kick connected beautifully with the face of the third, unbalancing him and turning his hard sprint into a drunken lumber. This coolness under assault, this bravery gave Komodo all the time he needed to get back on top, heaving one opponent over his shoulders and then stamping on his face. Another received a crushing double-handed blow to the top of his skull. The third caught a bullet.

Karin hopped back to the computer screen unperturbed. She finally unleashed her beast, watching it prowl, stalk and charge. The strands that led to SaBo's field system started to unravel, fraying by the second. She imagined the panic on the other side, the computer genius struggling to take it all in.

Another minute and she would take him down.

Komodo flung a hard drive at the next man that came through the door. Then, assuming his brief honeymoon period was over—all the mercs couldn't be that stupid surely—he took the fight to them, stepping over the threshold and outside the cyberwar room. The scene could be much worse. Only three more enemies faced him, all caught by surprise; two actually in the process of arguing with their leader.

Komodo raised his weapon and fired. Both rebels were knocked back hard by head shots, clattering over desks. The boss gained precious seconds in which to get off a shot. Komodo didn't have chance to dodge out of the way, and felt it whizz past his cheek. Interesting; if he'd darted to that side the bullet would have taken his face off. He rapidly closed the gap and grabbed hold of the last man's gun arm, twisting it roughly.

"Hate fuckers like you," he grunted and broke the arm. "You killed Pearson for nothing. And how many others?" He squeezed the broken joint until the man screamed himself into unconsciousness, and then bound the wrists with tape he found in a drawer.

"Let the British deal with you."

Karin saw her virus sidetracked at the last moment and felt her heart drop through the floor. It couldn't be. *No!* Sunnyvale was depending on her. As were the town's civilians and the huge attack team. Not to mention Drake. The CCTV and signal-jamming SaBo was employing simply had to be taken down.

Would SaBo purge his system?

No. The old hacker was too wily for that, plus he probably didn't want to be executed by Coyote's men for his failure. Karin saw his setup as the eyes and ears and defense mechanism for Coyote's army of mercs and its total destruction as a major lifesaver for all the British forces.

And Sunnyvale's SPEAR team's last desperate hope. It was all they had left.

Could she do it? The odds were certainly against her, racked high in SaBo's favor. She *had* to get inside.

Komodo returned. "Thanks for the help back there."

Karin held up a hand, barely daring to breathe.

One last chance, she thought. *One . . . last . . . chance . . .*

Something clicked in front of her. Confused, she leaned in closer, hardly able to believe what she was seeing.

"Oh my God," she breathed as all her screens lit up. "Look at the bloody hotel. We may be too late!"

CHAPTER THIRTY ONE

Kinimaka slammed the phone down and met Hayden's questioning eyes.

"Still nothing," he said. "All they know is that the tournament's still on. Drake and the rest are inside some hotel. And the Brits are about to charge."

Hayden rubbed at tired eyes. "Talk about a clusterfuck. But give Karin time. That girl will come through."

Kinimaka nodded. "I'm sure she will. The Hawaiian in me wants to lay back and hang loose, you know? The friend and comrade wants her to hurry the hell up."

"My dad felt the same about me."

Kinimaka's face fell. "Hay, I'm sorry. It's all just a little frustrating. We're usually on the front lines, you know? Fighting alongside the team. I feel a little . . . redundant."

Hayden stared down at her prone body, covered by a hospital sheet. "Join the club."

As if on cue, Smyth burst into the room, cellphone in hand. "Just got a call. You know we're still monitoring world events through our old HQ link? The system the CIA boffins set up? Well, we got a damn big hit. If the team were together we'd be all over this . . ." Smyth paused as several pings rang out from his cell.

Kinimaka frowned. "Is that more?"

Smyth looked a little embarrassed. "Not really. I may have sent one or two texts to Mai during the last few hours. Now that Karin's taken down part of Sabo's jammer it seems they're going through."

Ping! Ping . . . ping . . . ping . . . ping . . . ping . . .

"One or two?" Hayden asked with a straight face.

"Well, whatever," Smyth went on crossly. "Point is this: Watch!"

Kinimaka leaned forward as Smyth proffered the cell, careful not to let his bulk get in Hayden's eye line. He saw a room he recognized being invaded by men that moved fast and proficiently. He didn't believe his eyes.

"But that's—"

"Our *old* HQ," Hayden finished for him. "Shit, it doesn't matter that the place got shot to shit. Someone's after the hard drives and the information stored on them. How old is this video, Smyth?"

"It's not," Smyth barked. "It's real time."

"You gotta go! You gotta go now. Why the hell anyone would want those drives I don't know, but we have to stop them. Jonathan—" her voice broke a little. "Jonathan had them installed in tandem with his own system so he could work from both his office and the HQ. Maybe it's *his* drives they're after."

Smyth headed for the door. "Already on my way."

Kinimaka took out a cell of his own and followed. "Doesn't feel right," he mumbled. "Calling for back up. Just don't feel right."

Kinimaka raced through the streets of DC, acutely conscious they were headed back to the place where Romero died. Smyth would be even more aware. The traffic was thankfully sparse, the journey short. Smyth kept an eye on their surveillance camera through his phone link. Kinimaka reported on the progress of the backup team.

"We'll get there first," he said. "By two minutes."

"Long enough to count against us," Smyth rasped back. "Can't wait."

"Agreed."

They pulled up alongside the curb and jumped out. Smyth ran around to the back, popping the trunk and raiding the underfloor weapons' box for firepower. He handed Kinimaka a machine gun and a Glock, clips, a flak-jacket and smoke bombs.

His cellphone continued to ping.

Kinimaka inclined his head. "Might be best to turn that off, buddy."

Smyth growled, but complied. The two men went off at a dead run, knowing what to expect. Both of them had visited the old HQ recently to collect any data the global tracking systems might have picked up.

They hadn't expected the facility to be invaded over a week after being destroyed.

The back stairs led directly into the common room, the place where they'd all met to talk. Smyth crouched at the topmost landing.

"You ready?"

Kinimaka nodded. "Do it."

Smyth rose and paced forward at a controlled rate, gun held alongside his chin and pointed toward the enemy. He slipped inside the main door then paused, holding his breath. Kinimaka slid along beside him. They were ghosts, impressions of light and dark, mere shadows that flitted to and fro and made no noise.

Men hunched over computer terminals before them. Some were down on their knees. Smyth and Kinimaka stood silently over them, unseen, and performed a quick head count.

Outnumbered eight to two.

Smyth made the kill sign. Kinimaka nodded. They were not about to issue a warning to a superior number of mercs that had just broken into a secret, information-laden building armed with semis. Smyth fired first, his suppressed weapon making a popping sound and efficiently making three holes in three foreheads.

He moved as he worked. Kinimaka eased away to the right, keeping the positions of the remaining mercs at the front of his mind. Two double taps and another two bodies dropped. One of the mercs backed away, weapon pivoting, but Smyth took him down with a slightly messy neck shot.

Two left.

Kinimaka drifted again, stealing the distance between his adversary and himself away. Through a gap in the desks he saw a body, firing instantly. The man dropped. He looked over to Smyth, saw his comrade give a thumbs up.

"Got 'em."

Kinimaka rose. "Careful. I shot the last one in the collarbone. We need information."

Smyth grinned. "Me too! That means we got one each to interrogate. Hey, not bad for CIA, man. Not bad at all."

Kinimaka was experienced enough to understand such praise coming from an ex-Delta force soldier was rare and hard-earned. "Mahalo."

"Right," Smyth snarled at his captive. "Let's see what we're up against."

CHAPTER THIRTY TWO

Kinimaka didn't have to work hard to show his prisoner that he was a tad unhappy. Leaving Hayden alone—she actually had a CIA honor guard outside her room—the rest of his team in peril; the recent deaths and fighting the man-monster earlier that day, had all left him feeling more than a little edgy.

"I'm gonna ask you once," he growled, for once having a reason to make his bulk as large and intimidating as possible. "Why are you here? Who do you work for?"

The merc didn't even try to resist. Broken and reset bones were murder in his game. They slowed you down and got you killed. "Dudes' just recruited me," he blabbed. "Through some friend of a friend. No real IDs shown on either side. Man, it was real hush-hush, you know, but paid a boatload. All I know is I work for a group called the Pythians and they're bad shit, man. Real bad."

Kinimaka stared at him. This group, the Pythians, had been flagging up a lot recently. Of course, they wouldn't advertise their name if they didn't want people to know it. In warfare, you were always going to lose men to seizure and subsequent interrogation.

So what did that tell him?

"The guys in my unit talked a lot. Said they were a new group but big. Nobody knows who they are. Y'know, like the fuckin' Templars, or something. Wanna rule the world, you know?"

"I know the type," Kinimaka said with a touch of dry sarcasm. "What do these Pythians want?"

"Who knows, man? World peace? Civil war? Cats in space? Fuckin' fruit bats the lot of them. The guys told stories of Pandora's Box, the Lionheart and some mega-dude called Saint German, or something. All sorts of secrets, myths and crap. This Saint German guy is involved in the greatest mystery of all time." The merc spat. "Like I said—fruit bats the lots of them."

Kinimaka knew the man was blabbing without giving a single thing away. "And here?" he asked. "What exactly did you come for?"

Now the man's eyes dropped, the shoulders tensed. All the telltale signs of resistance. Kinimaka said nothing, but moved one step forward and planted his enormous boot on an outstretched hand.

"Hey. *Hey*! Wait, I'll talk. It's my first mission. I don't owe these bastards crap. The objective was the hard drives but one in particular. The bosses—they wanted the one that the Secretary of Defense used. You know, Jonathan Gates?"

"Yes. I know."

"No clue why. I kinda liked the dude myself."

Kinimaka removed his boot. "Keep talking."

The eyes dropped again. "I don't know any more, man!"

"Do you *want* to hear the sound of your own bones breaking? Is that what you want?"

"All right, all right. The op wasn't a smash and grab, it was an information steal, you know? A download. They wanted us to grab everything on Gates' computer that related to Stone."

Kinimaka squinted. "Who?"

"Bill Stone. General Bill Stone. The army guy."

Kinimaka stared at the merc. *The army guy*. The very man Gates had suspected to be involved in the hijacking of the original Odin doomsday weapon before it got blown sky high; the man Gates believed was traitorous in some if not all ways.

The man Lauren Fox had been about to work her own particular brand of magic on.

"What else?"

"That's it, dude. I swear. Christ, isn't that enough?"

Kinimaka moved away to confer with Smyth, both men tying the hands and feet of their captives before retreating. A quick discussion revealed their men spoke similar tales, probably with the odd tequila-induced embellishment.

Smyth tapped his weapon on the floor, handle first. "So what now? We can't exactly take this to the new Secretary. Our first act shouldn't be to accuse a General of treason."

Kinimaka indicated the pile of hard drives. "These idiots did our job for us. We take the drives. Let's see what Jonathan compiled first. And maybe . . ." He paused and tapped at his phone.

Smyth narrowed his eyes. "What?"

"Give me a minute. Hi, this is Agent Kinimaka." He reeled off a set of security codes, finally being put through to an inner switchboard. "Find Lauren Fox on a secure line for me," he said.

Smyth looked interested. "The hooker?"

"She's *not* a hooker." Kinimaka said without thinking, then clicked his tongue loudly. "Well she *is* a hooker. But she's *our* hooker. Ergo—she's not a hooker."

"Fuck me. I have no idea what you just said. Is that a Hawaiian proverb, man?"

Kinimaka blinked, remembering Hayden asking him the same thing once before during their original encounter with the Blood King. "I don't do proverbs, Smyth. I'm saying Lauren is part of the team so leave her alone."

"Oh, right. Well, next time just spit it out, okay?"

Kinimaka tuned him out as Lauren came on the line. "Listen," he said quickly. "We're secure, so speak freely. Jonathan once asked you to spy on . . . *somebody*. You didn't do it. Is the window still open?"

He knew the line was secure, but this was a source currently inside the Pentagon he was calling, after all.

Lauren didn't reply for a while. Kinimaka could hear her breathing. "I think so," she said at length. "At the time I thought not. But he hasn't stopped calling, trying to set something up. I'm pretty confident that my cover wasn't blown."

"Pretty confident?" Kinimaka said doubtfully.

"That's what I said."

"You believe you can set something up?"

"You mean—set *him* up?"

"That's what I mean."

"Hey, I'm a New York girl. I got confidence coming outta my ears, Mano. Come by the Pentagon sometime. We'll talk."

"Sounds good."

Kinimaka punched the end button and surveyed the room. "Let's get this thing started."

CHAPTER THIRTY THREE

Matt Drake faced off with Torsten Dahl. Mai faced up to Alicia. The air in the hotel lobby was electric, the tension a living, breathing animal with teeth and claws.

If they refused to fight, twelve civilians would be blown up and then Coyote and her men would barricade the half-full church and set it on fire. Then they would start going door to door with RPGs.

The army incursion wouldn't make it in time. Karin hadn't been heard from. Same story with Crouch.

The tournament was still on.

Drake nodded to Dahl. "Smile for the camera whilst I thump you into next week."

The Swede didn't look impressed. "Is that a Yorkshire way of saying you're scared?"

Drake threw a punch he knew would be deflected, struck out with a series of martial arts moves he knew would be defended. Dahl came back at him, gaining a punch to the arm and a bruise on the thigh. Drake doubled him over, but allowed him to fall back. To their right Mai and Alicia performed a similar dance, making it look good, but taking very little damage.

Within a few minutes the sugary tomes that would haunt Drake for the rest of his life drifted through the lobby.

"Stop pussyfooting around, boys and girls. This is where it gets real. I want to see some blood and guts or the next sound you hear will be Mr. John Featherstone's scream as his body parts have a disagreement and *split*. You hear me?"

Drake glared around the vast lobby. "We're out of options, folks. Her bloody computer guy has eyes and ears everywhere." He shook his head, remembering the band attached to his wrist. "Even monitoring our heartbeats."

"That's right," Coyote said just to drive her point home. "How exciting. My money's on the big Swede."

"I dunno." Alicia dropped into defensive mode. "I'm still fancying Beauregard."

Mai smirked. "The tights again?"

"It was in my face." Alicia grinned.

Mai blitzed her, employing several blows that brought her in close, then used elbows before spinning back out again. Alicia spluttered and held a hand up to her face. "Damn, if that turns into another black eye, you're history, Sprite."

"More like it," Coyote said sweetly. "And the men?"

Drake feinted and ducked, slamming a hard right into Dahl's midriff. The Swede's muscles were flexed, absorbing the blow. He stepped away and then came right back with a push-kick, surprising Drake and bruising ribs. The Yorkshireman threw caution to the wind, getting stuck in, and ran at his unlikely opponent, catching him around the waist in a bear hug and driving him backward.

Dahl's clenched fists crashed down onto his exposed back with a blow that would have felled a charging raptor. Drake's teeth clenched but he kept on pushing, the momentum driving him on, until he slammed Dahl into the wall that supported the staircase. The whole side of the structure juddered, plaster cracked, and there was the sound of splitting timbers.

Dahl grunted.

Drake stepped away, ducking as a fist whistled past his ear. Dahl somehow managed to grip one of the staircase's spindles just above his head and used it to gain leverage, kicking out and connecting with Drake's chest.

"Oof!"

Coyote's clapping echoed around the lobby.

Mai drove Alicia back against the reception desk, then ducked under a flurry of blows, raised the Englishwoman up, and deposited her hard on the polished surface. Cracks raced away to all sides like a crazy spider web. Alicia swiveled and slipped off, falling to her knees and striking low. Mai found her impetus upset and stepped aside, ready to drive again. Alicia jumped back up onto the desk in order to gain the high ground then yelled in surprise as it collapsed around her.

Fractured sheets of wood fell inward. The front of the desk collapsed. Alicia disappeared amidst the destruction, leaving Mai staring in disbelief.

Drake took a step and launched a high front kick at the Swede's chest, determined to stay on par. The blow was blocked but the force of it sent Dahl back against the staircase. This time the entire wall cracked. A hole appeared behind the Swede, revealing a dark space where the staircase's supports lived. Without thought, Drake strove to keep the Swede on the back foot, hitting him again and again around the chest—not the face or other vital areas—and driving him even deeper into the fissure.

Off balance, Dahl pinwheeled backward, striking support after support, smashing the timbers apart. Drake heard the staircase coming down before he saw it, but by then it was too late. The structure began to tumble down around him.

"Shit!"

Drake hit the deck, covering the back of his head with his hands. He heard Dahl grunting about dumb northerners somewhere among the collapsing construction up ahead. A heavy chunk of six connected risers smashed down inches from his feet. The main staircase almost seemed to slide off its moorings, slipping out into the lobby and leaving a spindly carcass behind. In the darkness near the back wall something sparked; a circuit blowing or shorting. Tiny flames flared into life.

Drake coughed and looked up. Dahl stood before him.

"Dickhead."

The Swede reached down with huge arms. Drake knew exactly what was coming but couldn't react in time. A second later he felt himself pulled up and lifted into the air; then he was in mid-flight, enjoying the air-time but not looking forward to the landing. He smashed down amidst a great splintering, remembering that there'd been a low wooden table where he now lay.

Shit, they were wrecking the place. Demolishing it.

Alicia rose from the wrecked desk. "A phoenix from the ashes," she said as she tried to maintain her dignity.

Mai eyed the vast desk she'd destroyed. "A dumb blonde from Essex," she returned.

Alicia held out a hand. "Just . . . wait. Wait until I get myself untangled from this shit." She picked her way carefully out of the mass of splintered and cracked wood, avoiding sharp edges, then gave an imperious flick of her hair.

"Okay. I'm ready."

Mai didn't waste time, painfully aware of Coyote's eyes and SaBo's careful monitoring system. She propelled Alicia into the warren of Egyptian artefacts, not only keeping up the onslaught but purposely giving the other woman more obstructions than she could handle. Sphinxes tumbled and crashed to the floor, their heads rolling across the Turkish rug. Alicia threw a display but Mai ducked under it. A short row of pillars, topped by objects, fell in unison like a tumbling row of dominos. Alicia caught Mai's lashing foot and twisted, making the other woman perform a three-hundred-and-sixty degree spin just to keep her attack at the correct pace. Mai executed the spin and came back around for good measure, slapping Alicia across the face with the sole of her other foot in mid-flight.

Alicia dropped the foot, shocked. "Shit. You're a goddamn Power Ranger. That's what you are."

Dust and falling shavings and other particles swirled all around them. Drake rose and staggered out of the remains of the table, almost falling, but used Alicia's back as a leaning post. As he eyed Dahl he saw the electrical fire that had started under the stairs.

"Ah, guys. That can't be good."

Flickering flames ran along wires and into circuit boards, spreading fast. Dahl ran at Drake, but the Yorkshireman slipped under his grasp, loping out of reach. To his left Mai, close enough to touch, grabbed Alicia and spun her around, then kicked her away.

Dahl delivered a weighty blow to Drake's ribs that left him gasping, stunned.

Mai sent the Swede a hard look, then jumped at him, instinct urging her to protect Drake. Her thighs grasped the Swede around the head, her arms balanced on the floor by his feet, and then she yanked him over. The Swede gave a yell of surprise and fell hard.

Alicia, losing her opponent, came at Drake, feinting before slipping around his body and grabbing his throat in a choke hold. Drake felt no slack in the powerful grip, corroborated by the fact that his face started to turn red.

He couldn't breathe.

Mai landed hard on Dahl's chest, driving her knees in. Her next strike landed on his right ear, rocking his senses. Her next was to his nose, making him see black spots. The final blow would come from stiffened fingers to the larynx; a strike that would hit like a knife.

Drake fell to his knees, almost blacking out.

The dust hung heavy in the lobby. Smoke from the fire began to billow. An explosion boomed out from below, the blast taking part of the floor with it. Still more wreckage plumed into the lobby, now licked with flames. Part of an upper floor collapsed, showering the lobby with debris, dust and bits of carpet; even bedside cabinets, a small TV, and a chair came crashing down.

Amidst the chaos the four fought. Drake recovered quickly, in time to reverse head-butt Alicia, breaking the choke hold, then used what little strength he had left to send a powerful punch at her cheekbone. The Englishwoman cried out. Drake fell back as she threw herself at him and caught her by her own throat just as she regained her hold on his own.

Eye-to-eye, they fought to survive. To be the last man standing.

Mai sent her throat jab but Dahl diverted it at the last second. His large hand struck her temple. Mai wavered. The Swede bucked, trying to throw her off, but the Japanese woman jabbed at his nervous system, making him fold with agony.

The fires burned all around them. The hotel's innards collapsed. In the intensity and the terrible heart-wrenching destiny and the heat of the moment, the final blows were struck.

SaBo couldn't believe his eyes. He stared at his computer screen, checking three times before he dared relate his finding to Coyote.

"My God, you will not believe this."

"Tell me." Sugary and confident.

SaBo checked again, trying to evaluate every circuit, keep that bitch Karin at bay, and assess his findings. The screens didn't lie.

"The damn place is a mess, but you can obviously see that. The monitors that show their life signs, the ones we clipped to them. Well, they've actually changed. Not as though they've been removed, which I installed a trip alert for, but genuinely. Authentically. Shit, I just didn't think they'd go that far."

SaBo watched in dumb amazement as, one by one, the red pulsing life signs that indicated the SPEAR team slowly winked out.

Until only one remained.

"They're dead," he said. "Monitors prove it. Life signs have flatlined."

Coyote sounded angry. *"All* of them?"

"No. No. There's one left. Only one left alive."

"Tell me." The anticipation was sickly.

"Drake," SaBo said. "Matt Drake."

CHAPTER THIRTY FOUR

Michael Crouch was having his best workout of the last ten years. Once, he'd been above the best—at first the young rookie trying to fit in and impress his peers, moving on to acceptance and respect. In the Army, the man that carried his load and looked out for his men was a man to admire, and Crouch had those qualities in abundance. Leadership values elevated him to the top, yes, but he knew the support of his team, his men, was the real backbone that kept him strong.

Now, having being chained to an office for more years than he could count, having allowed himself to lose that knife edge, he found himself back in the field. Trying to avoid young and seasoned mercs. Trying to save a small town and a great many civilians from those forms of terror the British intelligence and military services saved them from every day.

And now they were at the crux of it all. He wondered if Drake had found Shelly yet. *Coyote!* He berated himself. *Stop thinking of her as . . . something personal.*

Dark fields spread out to left and right. Crouch tried to retrace the route he'd used previously and soon found himself near the outskirts of town. There was no mistaking the British presence. Great floodlights revealed their HQ, unlit now, and choppers hovered nearby. Crouch hoped he wouldn't come up against some upstart of a sentry that might find it amusing to throw him into some makeshift prison. But he wasn't too worried. He possessed enough high-level, code-red passwords to wake the entire war cabinet.

The carnival lay ahead, with its big circus tent at the far end. Crouch decided to cut through, thus saving himself precious minutes. He doubted that many workers remained after last night, but imagined more than a few would have slept through the ruckus. As he moved, he kept an eye on the British contingent. The more he saw, the odder it seemed.

Helicopters whirring at speed. But no men, save for the odd figure standing around. Obviously he couldn't see through hastily erected tents, but . . .

It hit him.

The assault had begun. The British were on their way. Damn, he was only ten minutes away. If Karin hadn't taken SaBo's surveillance grid down, half these men were going to die for nothing. Crouch doubled his speed, feeling the burn in his lungs, the strain in places he'd never felt it before. As he moved he began to see shadows ahead; tall, thin shadows that existed in places they shouldn't be.

Coyote's mercs. Lying in wait inside and around the edges of the carnival. Lying in wait for the approaching liberators.

Crouch thought it through quickly; his sharp, strategic mind snapping it all together. Most likely the SAS would lead, negating the advantage the mercs currently possessed since it was clear the British Special Forces would sniff them out before a shot was fired. The only advantages for Coyote were SaBo's surveillance system, a defensive position, and foresight that this might happen, and . . .

. . . and the civilians.

Coyote was sacrificing these mercs and no mistake. No way would she want to be captured. Crouch knelt in the cold earth, the soft mound giving way like castles in the sand. In his left hand was a gun filled with a dozen bullets. The mercs weren't expecting an attack from the direction of the town.

Time to use it and hope to God the SAS didn't kill him. Wouldn't that be ironic?

Crouch stood. Instantly, the color of flames washed across his face as a nearby electrical point blew up. The SAS had already prepped the place. Mercs opened fire, seeing shadows. Crouch fired twice, dropping the easily identifiable mercs in their Kevlar and face masks. Once out of the shadow of rides, slides and sideshows, the random stands and mini-arcades, the generators and food stalls; the army of mercs shocked Crouch. There were more than he'd thought.

A lot more.

And they carried missile launchers. Grenades. They moved in formation. Before him, a mass of men capable of holding off the British forces moved out.

Crouch saw the British coming in the distance. He didn't see the SAS, but hoped they were reporting back. More incendiary devices went off. Bullets flew. The bigger rides started to shudder and shake as lead smacked into them.

Crouch realized he was superfluous. This battle was going down hard, right now. The British came from all angles except the town, firing at targets. Crouch, from his low vantage point, saw choppers rising over the heads of the running men.

C'mon Karin. C'mon Drake, he thought. One single needless loss of British life was one too many. *Give us an edge.*

CHAPTER THIRTY FIVE

Matt Drake emerged from the ruined hotel, staggering from side to side. The battle had not been kind to him. Ribs were bruised. Red marks covered his neck, testaments to how hard Alicia had squeezed. Dust covered his body from head to toe.

Coyote chuckled. "Now that's what I call a final fight, Matt."

The skies were bright, shining down on the town square. Coyote's mercs had thinned out. Drake heard the sounds of battle in the distance. He swallowed hard, not an easy feat with a mouthful of plaster, and licked his lips.

"They're coming for you."

Coyote indicated her dozen suited-up captives. "Let them come."

Drake stopped on the top step that led to the hotel doors. Billows of dust and smoke mushroomed through the shattered opening and windows at his back. He tried not to cough.

"How does it feel to be the last man standing? Your friends are dead. How does that feel, Matt? I'm sure Kovalenko—wherever he is—will be watching. Blood Vendetta fulfilled."

"We had a deal," Drake rasped, nodding at the captives. "Will you keep your word now, Shelly?"

The use of her name brought an open expression to her eyes. "I always do," she said, a touch regretfully. "I always have done. That's why we're in this fucked-up position, you and I."

She turned and, with a flick of her head, indicated that her lackeys should remove the nano-vests. Drake waited until they slithered to the floor.

"What now?"

"Well. You're not *actually* the last man standing, are you, Drake? There's also Beauregard." She gave him a sly smile. "And me. That's France versus England. An interesting matchup."

Drake flexed his already battered muscles.

"And let's not forget Japan," a lilting voice spoke out.

Coyote's eyes glimmered with confusion, her face slackening. "What? How?"

Mai Kitano emerged from the billowing dust; a white ghost.

Drake grinned. "C'mon Coyote. In what reality did you ever believe you could best me?"

Coyote shouted her fury. Her mercs raised their weapon and took aim. The townsfolk screamed and scattered or dived to the floor. Drake ran hard toward their nemesis, Mai at his back.

Coyote didn't wait. She didn't allow her lackeys to fire their weapons. She took off like a sprinter out of the blocks, running headlong toward Drake.

And in the middle of it all, from his position above the action on the roof of the town square, Beauregard Alain suddenly appeared, dropping down like a deadly snake.

Torsten Dahl's half-choked, disembodied voice came out of the fog. "Don't forget Sweden in that matchup."

And Alicia's too: "Is that Beauregard?"

CHAPTER THIRTY SIX

Drake met Coyote in battle, sending his first strikes against her vital areas. Unlike the previous struggle there would be no holding back in this one. They had all known the score from the moment they stepped into the hotel. Dahl had bruised a rib when he might have splintered it. Alicia had marked his neck when she could have broken it. Now, Drake had the chance to make Coyote pay for her mistake.

Drake ducked as Coyote came back at him; the two foes face to face. Shelly Cohen's face was unrecognizable, transformed into the wild animal she truly was at her core. The killer shone through for all to see, and Drake was still disturbed by it.

Coyote kneed him, pushed him away. A little distance opened up. Beyond her frame, her mercs fell to Beauregard, the French assassin a living scythe in their midst. The hotel continue to billow out smoke and emit sounds of destruction. Chopper blades whirred and clattered through the air. Explosions and gunfire made powerful rents in the dawn chorus.

Drake sensed an errant bullet whiz between them as he closed in on Coyote. It didn't matter. This was all about vengeance. Coyote knew what she'd done to Alyson; thus she knew it was always going to come down to this.

A blow landed on his temple, his bicep. He ignored the pain, stepping in and pummeling Coyote's midriff. He reached out to grab her throat, but she was wily and twisted away. She threw a succession of punches that Drake caught on his arms, deflecting the worst of the blows. She drove a knee into his stomach, taking the wind right out of him.

Drake fell to one knee, still deadly, by no means at a disadvantage with all the moves in his arsenal. His eyes never left those of his assailant and then he saw the shadow looming behind her.

Drake rolled away. Coyote, at the last instant, must have seen the shock or the figure reflected in his eyes, for she too threw herself aside. Beauregard, black-clad, reared up behind her but missed his deadly strike.

Drake scrambled away, creating space. Beauregard slipped between them. Coyote whirled and crouched in a ready position.

Three lethal adversaries, all poised to kill.

Explosions boomed out from the edge of town. Men screamed in earnest. Gunfire rattled. Drake saw the big wheel shudder.

Coyote didn't hesitate. "Damn, it's time!"

A moment later she was running, sprinting hard, not away from the battle at the edge of town, but right toward the heart of it.

CHAPTER THIRTY SEVEN

Dahl stumbled from the wrecked hotel, Alicia at his side. Like Drake, the two of them bore the wounds and bruises of battle and were covered in dust and debris. Smoke had blackened their faces.

Dahl had been afraid the civilian they freed earlier might have decided to loiter in the kitchens rather than chancing the outside world, and had insisted they check. Luckily, he'd fled.

Now Alicia surveyed the scene around the town square.

"Crap. I didn't expect that."

The area around them was empty, save for several inert bodies, all mercs. Away toward the right, heading downhill, she made out the figures of Drake and Mai. Ahead of them was Coyote in full flight.

"What the hell? And where's Beau?"

Dahl shrugged. "The assassin has shown her true colors," he noted. "Cowardly to the core. They lurk, they hide, they kill, never manning up and joining the fight. This is our town now."

Alicia set off. "I guess we should follow. Hey, what was all that about you dropping out of shiny school? Did Drake know?"

Dahl looked pained. "Nobody knew. It's my business alone. Let it go."

Alicia purposefully misunderstood. "That's the new mega song, right? Let it go? Have you seen the marines singing it on YouTube? Put a tear in my eye it did."

"No. I mean yes. I mean—that's not what I meant." Dahl sighed. "But you knew that, of course."

"Torsty," Alicia said. "Of all people, I get it. You should know that. If you don't wanna talk about it that's all right by me."

"Thanks." Dahl's reply was a grumble.

"Drake's observations are gonna be interesting though."

Dahl nodded glumly. "And so sharply perceptive, I'm sure."

Alicia laughed. "Yeah. That's always been his Yorkshire way. Perceptive as fuck."

Dahl sucked in his lips and said nothing. The decisions you made—simple or tough—they were the things that defined you. When faced with adversity you dug deep, finding the core to your heart and soul, and it was the choice you made at that time that changed you and turned you slowly and steadily into the person you would become. Dahl believed that was why hardships were visited upon men and women and their children.

To mold them.

If he'd chosen to leave and pursue an army career then it was that decision, among others, that had made him the man he was now. The craziness came from his rebellious side and he refused to reel that in. It was, after all, part of him.

The two were closing the gap now, the aftereffects of their tussle wearing off. Alicia even took a moment to untie the life sign monitor Coyote's mercs had made her wear.

"Won't be needing that anymore."

Dahl's face reverted to happy. "Oh yeah. Thank God for Karin Blake."

Alicia nodded. The 'battle to the death' had been their plan all along, totally reliant on Karin's ability to break through SaBo's defenses without the hacker knowing about it. When Crouch initially left Sunnyvale to contact Karin, one of the things he'd related was that particular plan. It had been up to her to make it work, to take the SPEAR team's monitors offline at the right time and fake their deaths, to fool one of the world's greatest hackers without him ever knowing it.

Karin had told Crouch she had just the weapon—a virus stored away in some redundant system. She'd just hoped she had the smarts to pull it off.

Dahl ripped his own monitor away. The sounds of battle—the mercs holding off the main incursion team—intensified ahead.

"We're walking into a war," Alicia noted.

Dahl glanced sideways at her. "So what else is new?"

CHAPTER THIRTY EIGHT

Drake raced headlong, recklessly, determined not to lose the Coyote. In his haste he did lose Mai. The Japanese woman, ever attentive, came across two mercs on their way out of town—deserters—and taught them that fleeing wasn't necessarily the best idea. When Mai looked around, Drake was gone.

Still, all roads led to the battle.

Drake crossed the muddy path that led through the carnival's gates and found himself inside the fence. Rides and stalls stood to his left and right, looking shabby, unpainted and tired in the light of day. A firefight raged ahead, stray bullets whickering everywhere. Mercs, Kevlar-suited special cops, and elite military units fought for ground.

But Drake knew the mercs were fighting blind. SaBo's surveillance blanket had been taken down. Karin had won the battle of the hackers.

Now it was his turn.

But where was—?

Coyote hit him from a blind spot, an elbow to the neck, sending him face-first to the floor. Drake rolled, eyes never leaving her feet. Did she have a gun? He glanced up, thankful to see empty, flexing hands. Coyote jumped at him, stomping hard, but Drake rolled again. His movement brought him up against another pair of legs—those belonging to a merc.

The man stared down in surprise. "What da fu—?"

Drake rose fast, delivering a gut punch. The merc folded, grunting hard. When the man's weapon came down, Drake grabbed it, reversed it, and smashed it across the man's head. Lights out.

Before he could bring the gun back around, Coyote was on him. They tumbled to the cold, muddy earth—face to face, body to body—arms tight around each other.

"You always wanted me this way," she breathed.

"The entire unit wanted you this way. But that wasn't *it*. You were much more than that. Didn't you know? Didn't you know that just your voice and your way, the ideal that was *you*, brought more men back alive than their bloody grenade launchers?"

"*I knew!*" Coyote screamed point blank into his face. "Of course I bloody knew!" She threw a punch that he turned away from and heard it squelch into the mud next to his face. "But I couldn't help it! *Don't you get that? I couldn't... fucking... help it!*"

She punched down again and again. The second one missed too, but the third caught him full on the nose, sending an arrow of agony into his brain. The fourth smashed into his temple, as did the fifth, and suddenly Drake was seeing stars.

"Shelly," he said. "Shelly!"

"Not Shelly!" Her fists continued to rage down upon him. "Not Shelly! Just a psycho who couldn't control it. A freak who learned to live with it."

Drake twisted and brought his hands up, but was fighting a losing battle. Coyote, on top, possessed all the power, all the leverage, and a lifetime of fury.

"I didn't want to be this monster!" she screamed. "I wanted to be Shelly! *Not fucking Coyote!*" And now tears fell from her eyes, dropping like beads of rain onto his bloody face.

Matt Drake gave it up. Not the battle, but the vengeance. He saw now the way it had all played out.

"Stop," he said, letting his hands fall to the sides and leaving himself wide open. "Stop then, Shelly. I don't want revenge on you. I want to help you."

Coyote's next blow fell hard, stopping a hair's breadth from the tip of his nose. The shock on her face transformed the animal within, restoring the woman he knew.

"I will help you," he said to the woman that had killed his wife and unborn child. "Let me."

For one second Shelly Cohen stared down at him. "Matt? I'm sorry. I—"

And then something hit her like a rocket; a black-clad figure that came out of nowhere and still fought for victory. Or was it something else?

Drake struggled upright. Beauregard and Coyote scrambled and rose, the Frenchman a millisecond quicker and thus gaining the advantage. Drake tried to shake off a foggy brain and blurred vision, and stepped up.

"Wait. Who the hell are *you* working for, Beauregard? Have they switched your orders? Told you to take *Coyote* out?"

The French assassin's face was hidden behind the feature-hugging mask. "The Pythians want you both," he said in his thickly accented voice. "All of you. They will remove anything that stands between them and the world. They will remove it with extreme and total prejudice." The man laughed. "Just wait and see."

With that he side-kicked Coyote's knee, forcing her to fall, and came around, tumbling across the ground toward Drake. At the last minute he swerved and threw out a lightning punch that Drake didn't even see.

But he felt it. The sudden agony in his throat made him reflexively send both his hands there, leaving the rest of his body open to violent, nerve-shattering attack. Beauregard was like Mai—one vital strike and you were dead.

Beauregard pounced.

And Michael Crouch took him down.

Drake flinched as Beauregard struck out, both fists flying, then let out a pent-up breath as Crouch landed on the man's exposed back. The Frenchman slammed into the dirt as if he'd been poleaxed, mud exploding out from under him.

Drake breathed hard. "Nice move." His throat was on fire.

Crouch shrugged. "I saw—" and suddenly disappeared. Drake blinked and saw Crouch hit the same mud as Beauregard, only the Frenchman was now standing upright, Crouch's neck in his hand, fingers pressed deeply into his victim's pressure points.

"You will die for that," Beauregard mouthed at Crouch.

"No!" Drake shouted, knowing he wouldn't make it in time.

The Frenchman flexed his fingers. Crouch screamed as if he'd been stabbed by a thousand daggers. His face turned instantly white, eyes glazing over.

And Drake could only watch as, unbelievably, *Coyote* leapt to the aid of her former boss. Her shriek of, "*Michael!*" was lost under the crunch of her body hitting Beauregard's. Crouch fell away, gasping. Drake ran to his aid.

"Your word," Drake heard Beauregard say to Coyote. "If your word can no longer be trusted, then you are no longer the Coyote."

Drake heard another cry as he patted Crouch's face. This one of twisted anguish.

Shit.

CHAPTER THIRTY NINE

He whirled, but Coyote was already on him, striking again and again, a pure killing machine. This time he made his punches tell; breaking ribs, jabbing at eyes and behind the ears, but it made no difference. Coyote was above it, beyond it, transported from a singular hell into a world of sudden chance—the world where she could again be Shelly—and now back to a life of pure torment and terrible desire. Choice made, she gave it her all.

Drake wilted slowly. When Beauregard appeared behind Coyote—a black angel of death—he knew the game was up.

Last man standing? Beauregard would win the day.

"I'm so sorry," Coyote muttered even as she pounded at him.

Beauregard's knife glinted with the fire of the rising sun.

The noise Drake would never have expected, the one that changed it all, was the roar of a motorbike. From the corner of his eye he saw a trial bike, ridden by Torsten Dahl, *ten feet off the ground*, soaring above them like the veritable bat out of hell. Dahl dangled from the seat and plucked the very blade from Beauregard's hands as he started to plunge it downward, then threw it back at the Frenchman.

Beauregard fell hard, avoiding the knife but hurting himself in the process. Dahl landed and turned the bike on a penny, mud and wet grass shooting from the spinning wheel. Coyote still struck out at Drake, but her attack was distracted.

Dahl shot between the two of them, blasting both their bodies and faces with dirt and thick sludge.

They fell back, opening a gap. Drake suddenly found himself with allies at his side. Standing in a line behind him had been Mai, Alicia and Crouch, now joined by Dahl on his bike.

Facing them were Coyote and Beauregard.

The titans of combat came together.

CHAPTER FORTY

All hell broke loose in the town of Sunnyvale.

The SAS had slipped around the flanks of the merc army and were among them. Paid mercenaries twisted every which way, fighting hard. SO units came at them from covered positions. Men fell, twisted and bled in the dirt. A high inflatable slide exploded and rapidly deflated among them, its flapping sides knocking three men off their feet. A funhouse, built on two levels of shaking walkways, distorting mirrors, screaming sirens and irregular steps exploded as two RPGs hit it. Timber and flame fired high into the air, debris shooting out like crazy fireworks, the whole thing lit like a blazing bonfire. Whatever snipers were inside died instantly.

Drake, Mai and Alicia ran at Beauregard and Coyote. Dahl revved his bike and shot forward like a bullet.

The big wheel, poised above the funhouse and littered with burning wreckage from its arms to its gondolas, shuddered and groaned for the second time that morning. Then, in slow motion, it started to tilt, the massive structure now leaning over. For a moment, as all eyes turned upward, it halted, hesitating as if deciding whether to hang on or give up the ghost. The morning was still for one precious instant, a span of tension and fear and a little regret, and then the circular edifice collapsed.

It came down among the men, bodies darting everywhere, some waiting until the last second and coolly stepping aside, others tying to gauge the structure's fall and being slammed into by those in a panic. Mayhem reigned. Those that still stood in the aftermath tried to pick off their enemies, some never losing a beat. Those that were injured or crushed yelled out to their colleagues and, depending on which side they were on, received immediate help.

Drake slid into Coyote, taking her legs. Alicia feinted past Beauregard, drawing his attention.

"Get a little closer, Beau. I got a ruler in my pocket and, man, do I wanna use it."

The Frenchman paused, as if confused. That gave Dahl all the time he needed to ram the speeding bike into his body, hurling him away from the handlebars. The Swede didn't let up on the throttle one bit, knowing they had to take such a dangerous enemy completely out of the picture.

When Beauregard landed, Alicia jumped atop him, just to make sure.

Drake had slid past Coyote, put a palm on the ground, and used it to spin his body back around. Now, as Coyote scrambled up, he hit her at the same time as Mai. The double-headed attack left the assassin lying on her back, winded and trying to catch her breath.

"Give it up," Drake said. "Tell your mercs to stand down. It's over."

Coyote spat at him.

"Shelly," Drake tried. "There's no need for any more loss of life."

Crouch joined them. "We protect our people, Shelly. Not sacrifice them."

Coyote snarled. "Shelly died when she was eight! When *I* made her torture her first small animal. Innocent girl, long lost. Poor girl. Poor parents. They knew when she changed. They knew when the killer took root. Only it was *me* who learned to control it. To feed it slowly and never get caught. If Shelly ever came back . . . the animal would destroy her."

Drake stepped back as Coyote kicked out and managed to regain her feet. Mai produced a pistol that she'd taken from a dead merc in anticipation of this moment.

"Stop," she said. "This is over."

Coyote smiled. The sugar-sweet tones slipped once more across Drake's senses. "The nano-vests were an experiment for the Pythians," she said. "In the event of my capture that was the last thing I was supposed to tell you. My job is over."

"Experiment?" Drake repeated. "What kind of experiment?"

"I don't know. When Kovalenko failed them in DC—he was supposed to put one on the President you know—it fell to me as the next person in line to try them out. My guess? It's nothing fun."

Drake felt his heart plummet like a falling star. "Kovalenko was working for someone? No way."

"The Pythians helped bankroll him when he couldn't get access to his money in prison. You think he did that? No way. They fine-tuned the op in DC. They gave him the drone that was used, the nano-vests."

"Before today I never even heard of the goddamn Pythians."

"You will," Coyote said. "Very soon. Their agenda is global and lengthy."

Mai waved her pistol. "Are you giving up?"

Coyote smiled a little wistfully. "Shelly will never let you take me alive."

Drake looked around: At the battle behind them that still raged; SAS troops darting in and out of enemy positions; police officers crouched behind the dead, using their bodies as shields as they picked off more of their opponents. A central stall caught fire as he watched, hanging prizes melting and popping. A food stand fell over, crushing an unlucky merc. Mud glistened across the entire scene. Beyond where the big wheel had stood was a rollercoaster and now, spectacularly, its central supports buckled, making the entire metal track warp.

The mercs had seen that they were losing, dying. Death didn't offer a pay packet, nor a second chance or day release. Not like the British penal system. Some of them were already surrendering.

"I don't see a way out for you, Shelly."

"Coyote," the woman growled. "Call me Coyote."

And she stepped back, pulling her jacket wide open, to reveal the nano-vest buckled to her chest. The light in her eyes was crazed but the look on her face was almost blissful.

"I'm so glad my torture is at an end," she said and detonated.

CHAPTER FORTY ONE

Drake flew backwards, slammed off his feet by the blast. Blood and other things struck his body and face as he went airborne. Coyote's lone hand slapped his cheek, thwarting him for the last time. Even as he bounced to the ground he knew that, in her final moments, Shelly Cohen had returned and made Coyote take that all important step back.

Any closer, and they would all have been dead.

His first job was to check on his teammates—all of whom were stunned and blooded but in good shape—and then turn to check on Alicia. The sight of her straddling Beauregard didn't really surprise him. He did a double-take when she threw a punch at the injured man though.

"You still softening him up?"

"Quite the opposite," Alicia said. "I think he likes it."

Mai groaned.

Alicia climbed off the prone Frenchman. "You gotta see this thing, Mai. The tights really don't do it justice. It's huuuu—"

Three soldiers mercifully approached them just then, shutting Alicia up as they waved their guns. Crouch raised his hands and diverted them, no doubt establishing protocols.

Dahl surveyed their surroundings. "Well, we lost Coyote and captured Beauregard. The Frenchman is a link to the Pythians. Could be worse. I wonder what happened to the hacker."

Drake clicked his tongue. "We learned only what they wanted us to learn," he said. "It's how and when we find out why that worries me."

Crouch turned to them. "We all have a rather large amount of explaining to do, but we're good here. Carry on."

Drake motioned for a phone. "We'll call Karin and Komodo and catch up with the guys in DC." He turned to Mai. "Surprised you haven't heard from Smyth."

"Phone's on silent," she said, fishing it out and then making a face. "Oh hell. Looks like he's filled it up."

"Damn. Well, we'd better call them first."

Drake made the call. As he did so he turned full circle and surveyed the fiery skies and the scorched earth; the place where his long-held nemesis, Coyote, had died; the bruised and bloody SPEAR team and Mai Kitano—his old past and future.

Full circle indeed.

CHAPTER FORTY TWO

A short while later, Matt Drake found himself seated in the quiet corner of a large, old-fashioned pub in the center of York.

The place held memories for him. Nostalgia seeped through the walls. He had taken Alyson here. Even met Ben Blake here. Pain, sorrow and the memory of old mistakes hung like the shadows of ancient ghosts inside, but there was a certain happiness too. The pub held infinitely more good memories than bad.

On this day he sat with more friends. Mai, Alicia and Dahl. Michael Crouch. Karin and Komodo. Mai was upbeat but still reserved, the shadow that had followed her back from Tokyo well and truly returned. Alicia currently existed in a state of extremes—one moment buoyed by excitement and cracking one-liners and looking dangerous, the next hanging her head glumly as she thought no doubt of Lomas and the bikers, and where the path to her home might now lie.

Crouch imparted more news than he was probably allowed to. Karin and Komodo reported all they knew and told them of SaBo's fate. The hacker had fled at the first sign of trouble and hadn't resurfaced. Drake didn't worry. In this game they came across the same people again and again, and when they next met SaBo—they owed him a little personal hacking time of his own.

Hayden, Kinimaka and Smyth had reported in. The Pentagon appeared to be their new home. Drake rolled his eyes. Could they be under closer scrutiny? Especially now that Kinimaka and Lauren Fox were in the early phases of launching an entirely new operation against General Stone.

He had a feeling they were standing at a crossroads. The way back was littered with mixed memories and defining moments. The roads either side led to nowhere; a stagnant invariable path to dissolution. It was the way ahead that offered a vista of possibility.

Only in moving forward and facing new challenges could Matt Drake hope to survive.

And on the road ahead something big was looming. Something immeasurable, on the grandest scale yet.

He wanted to be there for that party.

"Not thinking of retiring now are you?" Crouch asked, noticing the depth of his concentration.

"Furthest thing from my mind," Drake said. "Coyote is dead. That lifts a weight from my shoulders, yes, but I actually pitied her at the end. I wanted Shelly back. If anything, I miss that girl."

Crouch smiled pensively. "Me too."

"Other things are coming," Drake said. "It will never end." Mai had spoken a similar sentence to him a long time ago, back when Kennedy was still alive.

"I know. That's one of the things I wanted to talk about."

Drake sensed something coming. "Of course, Michael."

"The Ninth Division is no more. Defunct. Of course, a new department will stand in but I have no interest in that. All my life I've wanted to pursue a dream, an ambition. It appears that now I'm in a position to do exactly that."

Drake smiled. "Sounds good. What kind of dream?"

Now Crouch looked slightly embarrassed, the first time that Drake had ever seen him so. "It's okay," the Yorkshireman said quickly. "You don't have to—"

"No, no," Crouch said quickly. "I want to. I have to, actually. You see all my life I've had this, largely secret, love for archaeological mysteries and ancient unsolved riddles. I guess you could call them cold cases, but ice-cold really. Frozen over. I'm not talking about old gods or Alexander the Great or the plagues of Egypt. I'm talking Aztecs, Incas, Mayans—the civilizations that came and went and left a million stories behind. Even the pirates, the stories they traded and told were pure gold dust." Crouch was speaking faster and faster, warming to his subject. "Real, living treasures that you can touch and discover. I want to form a team dedicated to searching for these treasures . . . and I have a backer."

"You do? That's fantastic."

"He provides the money. We get paid a wage. A good one. I have so many government contacts both here and around the world I need a book the size of the Bible just to keep track of them. Wheels can be greased, favors met."

Drake grimaced a little.

"It's what makes the world go around, Matt. Politics. Business. Commerce. Banking. The favors, the special invites, the small concessions. Negotiation is as much a currency as banknotes. In any case, I can get us access to a country and its more interesting parts through my contacts. Our benefactor has the money. Now all I need is a team."

Drake blinked rapidly. "Oh. Are you trying to ask *me?*" he blurted. "Sorry, I didn't realize. Us Yorkshire folk need it laid out in plain English. We're not that good on the uptake."

"Actually no." Crouch grinned. "I was asking *her.*"

He turned toward Alicia, who'd been listening in on their conversation. An expression of surprise was soon covered by a victorious leer.

"In yer face, Drakey!"

Crouch winced a little. "Her qualities are unmistakable."

Drake nodded seriously. "Alicia is the best teammate and companion anyone could ever hope for."

Crouch nodded. "That's what I thought."

Alicia stared down at the table. Her lips moved but nothing came out, as if the emotion had choked her words. Seconds passed. When finally she met Drake's gaze the slight sheen in her eyes spoke for her.

Crouch leaned forward. "Will you join me, Alicia?"

"I will," the Englishwoman said. "I will. But not indefinitely. My options are always open, Michael, so that if the something I've been looking for presents itself then I'm free to take it. I'll also have to talk to the bikers. And SPEAR."

Drake recognized the craving in those words, the desire that Alicia never let go. A free spirit, she would always follow the road, searching, seeking for that one thing she might never find.

A family.

"And of course you can call on her. And us. Anytime," Crouch told Drake, and now the rest of the table who had all tuned in.

Alicia said, "You guys have been awesome. The best soldiers, the best friends. The best of everything. Even you, Mai," she added with a laugh. "But I have to keep searching. Once a rebel always a rebel. Away with the clouds. Riding into the sunset. That's me. Look for me at the break of dawn, the dying of the day. That will be me—saluting you."

And she stood up, trying to hide the emotion she felt, no doubt trying to find that one last memorable quip.

"I'll say my proper goodbyes to SPEAR. Oh, and if I could maybe interrogate Beauregard? Three or four minutes of hard work and I should get what I need."

CHAPTER FORTY THREE

Tyler Webb sat alone behind his great desk, staring out of the enormous picture window that, due to the building's height, gave him a clear and wonderful view of the Falls. Such a grand view came at an equally grand premium, but Webb and his fellow Pythians sat on more riches than they could squander in a thousand lifetimes.

The Pythians were growing; becoming notorious, mysterious. Now they had a second layer of protection—a tier of first-degree members—each one powerful and wealthy in their own right. Not one of them knew who the puppetmasters were. Their army was growing. Security levels were extraordinary and would only increase in both physical and cyber strength. They would need the extra layers. Their recent failed operation in the heart of Washington DC was proof of that. Do-gooders were always happy to thwart them at every turn, laying their very lives in the line, for what? Glory? Duty? Certainly not power or money.

Webb didn't understand the lower masses at all.

Webb now allowed himself the luxury of respite. Goals and ambitions flooded his mind, crowding in. It would all start with Pandora, very soon. London, Paris and Los Angeles would pay a high price. After that, more attacks would come, some covert and deep, others as obvious as the destruction of a small town. The Pythians would worm their way into the infrastructure of the world, corrupting and betraying everything until they held every string that controlled every puppet, every red button that might start a war.

And above it all one single quest. One overwhelming objective.

The greatest unsolved mystery of our time:

Le Comte De Saint Germaine.

THE END

Please read on for some exciting information on the future of the Matt Drake world.

I sincerely hope you enjoyed reading Matt Drake 8—*Last Man Standing*—as much as I enjoyed writing it. The Coyote confrontation has been a long time coming, I know, so good to get it out there. Now we can move on to bigger things!

As you can probably guess, and for those that haven't yet checked my website, the news is that starting in December 2014 with *Aztec Gold*, Alicia Myles will get her own spin-off series, probably consisting of three books because, after that, a devastating event will force her to return to her SPEAR family . . .

And the biggest news yet—the next Drake, part 9, will be released in March 2015 and will be a 'crossover' novel, longer and bigger and more exciting than anything that has come before. The SPEAR team are joining the Disavowed and Alicia's new crew to take on the Pythians. It may surprise you to know that I have already completed 80% of the research for this book and intend to start writing over the summer.

Chosen 2 to be released September 2014!

As ever, e-mails are always welcomed and replied to within a few days. If you have any questions just drop me a line.

Please check my website for all updates—www.davidleadbeater.com

Word of mouth is essential for any author to succeed. If you enjoyed the book, please consider leaving a review at Amazon, even if it's only a line or two; it makes all the difference and would be very much appreciated.

Printed in Great Britain
by Amazon